"I have an idea that Bradbury's work would have given Edgar Allan Poe a peculiar satisfaction to have written them himself."

—*Somerset Maugham*

"Bradbury's dramas are admirable and curious and disturbing."

—*Sir Alec Guinness*

7

RAY BRADBURY

DINOSAUR TALES

RAY BRADBURY
DINOSAUR TALES

A
Byron Preiss
Book

Bantam Books
Toronto * New York * London * Sydney

To Willis O'Brien
Who Animated the Beasts in *The Lost World*
in 1925, and So Changed My Life, Forever.

DINOSAUR TALES
A Bantam Book / June 1983
FIRST EDITION

Cover illustration by William Stout
Cover and book design by Alex Jay
Mechanical production by Susan Hui Leung

ISBN 0-553-01484-6

Library of Congress Catalogue Card No. 82-45954

Published simultaneously in the United States and Canada

Bantam Books are published by Bantam Books, Inc. Its trademark, consisting of
the words "Bantam Books" and the portrayal of a rooster is Registered in U.S.
Patent and Trademark Office and in other countries. Marca Registrada. Bantam
Books, Inc., 666 Fifth Avenue, New York, New York 10103.

PRINTED IN THE UNITED STATES OF AMERICA
0 9 8 7 6 5 4 3 2 1

CONTENTS

FOREWORD

I saw my first living dinosaurs at the tender age of five. There they were, in the darkened cinema, parading and fighting through the prehistoric jungles on top of a great cliff. The visual engraving on my brain cells was unerasable. As far as I was concerned *The Lost World* of 1925 was true in every detail.

Some years later the original *King Kong*, with its vivid sound effects and exciting and "outrageous" music score was the final catalyst that made me decide that extinct animals must have some place in my life's work.

Unknown to me at the time, and several thousand miles away in Waukegan, Illinois, another equally impressionable young soul, also named Ray, reacted very much in the same way.

It was the dinosaur that was responsible for our first meeting at the Los Angeles Science Fiction League, and the long friendship that followed. It was the dinosaur that was our prime subject of discussion on the telephone, charging back and forth over the thin wires for long hours, waiting to be born in some new epic which was to be the greatest prehistoric film of all time. Somehow it never came off, but the enthusiasm generated kept each of us going for years after.

Ray pursued the path of the written word, finally to become one of the world's most admired writers in his field. The other Ray, myself, took the path of the moving visual image—the cinema.

It was "The Fog Horn" that brought us briefly together for one film project, *The Beast from 20,000 Fathoms*, out of which probably came the inspiration for "Tyrannosaurus Rex." Hopefully the Fates have in store another subject, yet unborn, that will bring us together professionally once again.

Here, for the first time in one volume, are all of Ray Bradbury's wonderful and unique dinosaur tales, new and old. They stretch the imagination, excite wonderment, and above all, give one hours of stimulating entertainment.

Ray Harryhausen

INTRODUCTION

At dinner one night, some years ago, someone asked each of us to name, in order of importance, our Most Favorite Subjects in All the History of the World! "Dinosaurs!" I cried. Followed swiftly by, "Egypt. Tutankhamen. Mummies!"

To bulwark my selections, I recounted a short tale about my own life as a twelve-year-old genius-in-the-bud. Telling my friends I was off for a life as a radio actor, I trotted down to the local station in Tucson, Arizona, hung about friendless, rootless, emptying ashtrays, running for Cokes, and exerting my own peculiar animal magnetism. Within two weeks, I wound up On The Air, reading the comics to the kiddies every Saturday night. Payment for same?

Free tickets for *King Kong* and *The Mummy*.

I was the richest boy I ever knew.

For doing what I loved to do, how nice that God, and the station manager, handed me passes to rub elbows with prehistoric monsters and dead Egyptian kings!

When I had finished saying all this, there was an instant revision of Lists at our table. Men and women, of all sizes, shapes, colors and ages, had to agree I had hit on Subjects Number One and Two.

But, especially One.

Dinosaurs.

For, as I put it to my friends:

"If, this very instant, a stranger rushed into this room crying, 'My God, there's a dinosaur outside!' what would you do?"

"Run out," everyone admitted, "and look!"

"Yes," I said, "even though you were absolutely sure it couldn't be true. How come, though, you would leap and run like that? Because you hoped for a miracle. In your secret heart of hearts you wanted brontosaurus, tame of course, to come back in the world.

"In fact," I added, turning to a television producer who had asked me, earlier, what I would like to write for television, "if you gave me prime time, and a few dollars,

there's nothing I'd write better than a show called *Dinosaurs! Roots*? That was watched by only fifty or sixty million people. Our *Dinosaurs* would rampage the country and grab every eye. Please pass the pteranodons."

Of course, nothing ever happened. I got everyone at dinner to admit they'd love to see such a television special, and the shared feeling was that dinosaurs were just about the greatest children of history, but the network executive never called back. I think he awoke the next morning blaming the wine.

Still, this late in time, my opinion remains: Dinosaurs and Tut. I haven't as yet figured out what should be in third place. Could be the Moon. Or Mars. They *almost* make it. But Stegosaurus makes it first.

Maybe because he's underfoot. We can see and touch and think on the bones that lie before us, along with the eggs, long since concretized, from which they ambled ten thousand million mornings ago. The Moon and Mars are absolutely real, but only a handful of men have touched one, and only our space-traveling cameras have eyed the other. When we walk on both, as most certainly we shall, perhaps those worlds will crowd Tut and pterodactyl at the tape.

But as for now I accept the fact, and proclaim it quietly, that without dinosaurs my life would have been nothing at all. Dinosaurs started me on the track to becoming a writer. Dinosaurs helped push me *along* that track to acceptance. And a dinosaur who fell in love with the sound of a lighthouse foghorn in a story called "The Fog Horn," which I wrote and published in 1950, changed my life, my income, and my way of writing forever.

In this story, which was the basis for the film, *The Beast from 20,000 Fathoms*, I allowed my gathered love for such beasts to speak out; that drew the attention of John Huston in 1953. He read the tale and sympathized with the plight of a monster who took the melancholy cry of the foghorn for the mating call of yet another lost beast. Huston sensed the ghost of Melville in the whole, and called me in to write the screenplay of *Moby Dick*.

16   RAY BRADBURY

What Huston sensed, of course, was not Melville but the influence of Shakespeare and the Bible on me. And since the Bible and Shakespeare yanked the White Whale full-blown from Melville's brow, it all ends the same. I got the job, wrote the script, and watched as Melville and his beast of prehistory settled into my life with vast tonnages and permanence.

So, you see, the dinosaurs that fell off the cliff in *The Lost World*, that ancient 1925 film, landed squarely on me, as did *King Kong* when I was twelve. Squashed magnificently flat, breathless for love, I floundered to my toy typewriter and spent the rest of my life dying of that unrequited love.

Along the way I met another young man, exactly my age, with exactly the same love, if not to say lust. For those prehistoric creatures paced his days, and stirred his nights. The young man's name was Ray Harryhausen. He was building, and animating with stop-motion 8 mm film, a family of dinosaurs, in his backyard garage. I visited the family often, handled the beasts, talked for hours, many nights in many years, with my friend, and we agreed: he was to grow up and birth dinosaurs, I was to grow up and dialogue them. And it came to pass.

The Beast from 20,000 Fathoms was the first and only film we shared together. Not a great film, not even a very good one, but the start of two careers that finally took his motion pictures, his beasts, and my books, into some of the farthest corners of the world. Culminating with the night, a year ago, when I introduced Harryhausen at a special screening honoring him, at the Motion Picture Academy of Arts and Sciences. As I finished my introduction, Fay Wray, the heroine of the 1933 version of *King Kong*, ran out of the audience, grabbed and hugged us both, and put the capper on two lives that had started with simple direct loves in museums, movie houses, and garages, a long time ago.

Along the way, Harryhausen and I had to put up with a lot of fly-by-night, round-heeled, always opinionated and always wrong pardon-my-feet-on-the-table produc-

ers. I became so enraged with the way one of them treated Ray that I wrote the enclosed story "Tyrannosaurus Rex" to restore my sanity.

Right now is confession time. Some thirty-odd years ago, Ray Harryhausen, my wife Maggie, and I attended a performance of *Siegfried* with the then eminent tenor Jussi Björling performing the title role. We went, of course, not to see Siegfried, or to hear the music, which was of course glorious. We went to see—God bless our lost, sweet souls—Fafner, the Dragon.

I realize, in admitting this, that Harryhausen and I will probably go on most opera lovers' lists as the coarsest, most unthinking, most damnable *Siegfried* attendees in history. I accept the damnation and live with the guilt. Nevertheless, there we were, the three of us, in the lower left hand side of the balcony, waiting for what seemed nine hours, and was probably only eight, for Fafner to appear.

He appeared all right. I saw an inch of his left nostril, Maggie saw one of his whiskers, and Harryhausen saw only the vast cloud of steam Fafner gave off in his brief "aria" before he vanished.

For, you see, our seats were so devilishly positioned, and the scenery onstage so cleverly built, that at least one-third of each audience never saw the brute clear. We were part of that one bereft third.

Stunned, Ray and I looked across my wife at each other. The long wait through the admittedly wondrous music was all for nothing.

Shortly thereafter, we beat a retreat to the foyer, and thence, defeated and disconsolate, home.

Heading west toward the sea, a great car passed us carrying, in the back seat, a dark-haired queen, Elizabeth Taylor.

She was no consolation.

Though I never saw Fafner, I've continued to seek his cousins and the fantasies around them in libraries and bookshops. My love of these creatures is only equalled by my love of book illustration.

During the past forty years, when most American art galleries stood empty of all but those boring drip-dry paint-by-the-zeros abstracts, I took refuge in the bright arms of the Pre-Raphaelites. I raced backward through London and Paris, with Gustave Doré and Grandville, to knock heads with John Martin and try to replan the morals of Gin Lane and Fleet Street with Hogarth, or frolic in Louis' court with Callot. I was satisfied by nothing less than story, symbol, metaphor as found in all their works. Goya drove me to war, sat with me at bullfights, rode me on witch-brooms, and I was never the same. I came reeling out of most twentieth century art galleries, as one fresh from a Chinese dinner, wondering why I was hungry an hour later.

It follows then that when this book's editor showed me illustrated samples of these glorious beasts, I could not resist. The ghost of Harold Foster, who drew Tarzan for six years back in the early 1930s spoke to me. It said: Remember my dinosaurs that trudged your midnight bed and flew your ceiling skies! The ghosts of the creators of Buck Rogers and Flash Gordon said just about the same thing. My comic-collections, still gathered and waiting in my basement, fifty years later, reminded me of my first, art-oriented passions. Dulac, Tenggren, and Rackham raised this child from the crib on. No wonder I cried, "Aye!" when I saw the work published herein by Bil Stout, Steranko, Moebius, David Wiesner, Overton Loyd, Kenneth Smith and Gahan Wilson.

The other stories and poems collected here were written at one time or another during the years when, of a morning, or late afternoon, or some midnight, I suddenly asked myself what I would dearly like to write about, right *now*? The answer was, of course, "Dinosaurs!"

These are all *What If?* stories or poems. What if a dinosaur really did become enamored of a foghorn? What if we could travel in time and run back to hunt the prehistoric beasts? This last was an experiment I tried in 1950. I simply sat down to my typewriter one morning, with no idea where I would wind up, and hammered

together a Time Machine, and shot my hunters back a few million years to see what would happen. Three hours later, after a butterfly had been stepped on, making it one of the first, and unconscious, ecology stories, the tale was done, the beast slain, and all political history changed forever.

"Besides a Dinosaur, Whatta Ya Wanna Be When You Grow Up?" evolved from a similar simplistic concept. Having been a boy who wanted to wake up one morning with dragon teeth, I simply tossed the shuttle into my typewriter, and let the aging boy spin out his possibly frightful dream.

As for the dinosaurs dancing on the sandy shore? I have attended the ballet at least four hundred times in my life, and have seen quite a few lumbering beasts. Beyond that, my frolicsome animals are probably first cousins to the hippos, ostriches, and alligators that outraged us to joy, long ago, in *Fantasia*.

And as for my future plans? I am writing the libretto for a space-traveling opera titled *Leviathan 99*. In it, I move the Moby Dick mythology beyond the stars. The opera dramatizes the arrival of a Great White Comet that visits our basement part of the universe once each forty years. My equivalent of Ahab, the captain of a star ship, goes out to attack the Comet which destroyed his sight when he was a young man new to space. The opera is, of course, dedicated to Melville. In it, the Beast may have changed its form, but not its essence, its terror, its magnificent beauty. Deep in its incredible soul, it speaks with the heart of a boy who fell in love with just such beasts and wanted to run and live with them, fifty-seven years ago.

The boy shouted one word. The Great White Comet merely echoes it:

Dinosaurs, of course.

Dinosaurs!

Ray Bradbury
Los Angeles, August 12, 1982

RAY BRADBURY
DINOSAUR TALES

Besides a Dinosaur, Whatta Ya Wanna Be When You Grow Up?

"**A**sk me a question, okay?"

Benjamin Spaulding, aged twelve, had spoken. The boys, strewn on the summer lawn around him, didn't so much as blink an eye or wag a tail. The dogs, strewn with them, did just about the same. One yawned.

"Go on," said Benjamin. "Someone ask."

Maybe it was staring at the sky that made him say it. Up there were great shapes, strange beasts traveling who-knows-where out of who-knew-when. Maybe it was a growl of thunder beyond the horizon, a storm making up its mind to arrive. Or maybe this made him remember the shadows in the Field Museum where Old Time stirred like those other shadows seen last Saturday matinee when they reran *The Lost World* and monsters fell off cliffs and the boys stopped running up and down the aisles and yelled with terror and delight. Maybe—

"Okay," said one of the boys, eyes shut, so far deep in boredom he couldn't even yawn. "Like—whatta you wanna be when you grow up?"

"A dinosaur," said Benjamin Spaulding.

As if on cue, thunder sounded on the horizon.

The boys opened their eyes.

"A *what*?!!"

"Yeah, but *besides* a dinosaur—?"

"No," said Benjamin. "No other job worth having."

He eyed those clouds which moved in titanic shapes to eat each other away. Great legs of lightning strode over the land.

"Dinosaur—" whispered Benjamin.

"Let's get *outa* here!"

One dog led the way, the boys followed, snorting. "Dinosaurs? Ha! Dinosaurs!"

Benjamin jumped up and shook his fist. "You be what *you* wanna be, I'll be *mine!*"

But they were gone. Only one dog stayed, and he looked nervous and miserable.

"Heck with them. Come on, Rex. Let's eat!"

But just then the rain arrived. Rex ran. Benjamin stayed, looked proudly this way or that, head high, not minding the drench. Then, with miniature majesty, alone but wet and wondrous, he stalked across the lawn.

Thunder opened the front door for him. Thunder slammed it tight.

Self-made described Grandpa. Trouble was, he often said, shoveling in the chicken and spading in the apple pie to tamp it down, he had never decided what to make of himself.

So he had kind of run up a ramshackle life out of one-part railroad engineer, retired early to become town librarian, retired early to run for Mayor, retired early from that without ever starting. At present he was full-time operator of a Print Shop downtown and a dandelion wine press in the anti-Prohibition cellar of Grandma's boarding house. Between shop and cellar, he prowled his vast library which spilled over into dining room, halls, closets, and all bedrooms adjoining, up or down. His multitudinous hobbies included collecting butterflies trapped and kept on auto radiator screens, flower intimidation in a garden which refused his thumb, and grandson watching.

Right now, said watching was like buying a ticket for a volcano.

The volcano was inactive, seated at the noon table. Grandpa, sensing some hidden eruption, napkined his mouth and said:

"What's new out in that great world today? Fallen out of any flora lately? Some fauna, mad bees that is, chase you home?"

Benjamin hesitated. Boarders were arriving like cannibals and leaving like Christians. He waited for some new cannibals to start chewing, and then said:

"Found a lifetime job for myself."

Grandpa whistled softly. "Name the occupation!"

Benjamin named it.

"Jehoshaphat." Grandpa, to gain time, cut himself another chunk of pie. "Great you decided so young. But, how you go into training for that?"

"You got books in your library, Gramps."

"Chockful." Grandpa toyed with the crust. "But I don't recall any How To books dating from the Jurassic or the Cretaceous, when killing was the fashion and nobody seemed to mind. . . . "

"You got billions of magazines in the cellar, Grampa, half a zillion in the attic." Benjamin turned his flapjacks like pages, seeing the wonders. "Got to have nine hundred ninety pictures of primeval times and the stuff that lived there!"

Trapped in his awful habit of never throwing anything out, Grandpa could only say, quietly, "Benjamin—"

He lowered his eyes. The boy's parents, when he was ten, had vanished in a storm on the lake. They and their boat were never found. Since that time, various relatives had had to go down to the lake to find Benjamin yelling at the water and shouting, where was everyone and why didn't they come home? But he was down at the lake less often these days, and more often in the boarding house here. And now—Grandpa frowned—in the library.

"Not just any old dinosaur," Benjamin interrupted. "I'm out to be the best!"

"Brontosaurs?" suggested Grandpa. "They're nice."

"Nope!"

"Allosaurus, now, you take allosaurus. Pretty as toe-dancers, the way they kind of *sneak* along—"

"Nope!"

"Pterodactyls?" Grandpa was in fever now, leaning forward. "Fly high, look like those pictures of kite-machines drawn by Leonardo, you know, da Vinci."

"Pterodactyls," Benjamin mused, nodding, "are almost Number One."

"What is, then?"

"Rex," whispered the boy.

Grandpa glanced around. "You call the dog?"

"Rex." Benjamin shut his eyes and called out the full name. "Tyrannosaurus Rex!"

"Hot diggety," said Grandpa. "There's a name that rings. King of 'em all, eh?"

Benjamin was lost in time, mist, and sump-water trackless bogs.

"King," he whispered, "of 'em all."

He blinked his eyes wide, suddenly.

"Got any ideas, Gramps?"

The old man flinched under that pure sunfire stare.

"No. Er—just let me know what you find. In your research. . . ."

"Yay!" Taking this as approval, Benjamin vaulted from his chair, shot toward the door, froze, and turned. "Besides a library, where do you put in for it?"

"Put *in*?"

"Firemen put in at fire stations to train. Locomotive engineers put in at depots to learn. Doctors—"

"Where," said Grandpa. "Where does a boy go to graduate summa cum laude in First Class A-1 Lizard?"

"*All* that!"

"Field Museum, maybe. Full of bones from God's lower attic. Dinosaur college, boy! *Take* you there!"

"Gosh, Gramps, thanks! We'll be so happy, we'll run up and down, yelling!"

And—bang! the front door slammed. The boy was

gone.

"I bet we will, Benjamin."

Grandpa poured more syrup in patterns of golden light and peered down into the bright stuff, wondering how to douse a boy so full of fire.

"I bet we will," he said.

A great mad beast arrived, a great wild monster took them away. The train, that is, to Chicago, and Benjamin and Grandpa on it, in the belly of the beast, as 'twere, trading smiles and shouts.

"Chicago!" cried the conductor.

"How come," Benjamin said, frowning, "he didn't mention the Field Museum?!"

"*I'll* mention it," said Grandpa. And, a few minutes later, "Here it *is!*"

Inside they moved under murals of beasts to gape at monsters so dandy it knocked your wind out. Here they marveled at lost flesh, there they gasped at refound-restrung skeletons, hand in hand, wonder in wonder, young joy leading old remembrance of joy.

"Gramps, you ever notice? Look! This whole darn great place, and no guys, no folks from Green Town here!"

"Just you and me, Benjamin."

"Only folks I remember from home being here, a long time ago was"—the boy's voice faded to a whisper—"Mom and Dad. . . ."

To keep the moment from slopping over, Grandpa cut quickly in: "They sure did love it, boy. But now, look! Come on!"

They trotted over to be amazed, stunned, and awed by a pride of nightmares painted by Charles L. Knight.

"Man's a poet with a brush," said Grandpa, teetering on the brink of this Grand Canyon of Time. "Shakespeare on a wall. Now, Benjamin, where's that big dog, Rex, you been hankering on?"

"*That* skyscraper! That's *him!*"

They went to stand under the vast shape, their eyes playing silent tunes on the long xylophone necklace of bones.

"Wish we had a ladder."

"Climb up like mad dentists and tell him to open wide?"

"Ain't that a *grin*, Grandpa?"

"Similar to my mother-in-law at our wedding. You want to perch on my shoulders, Ben?"

"Could I?"

On Grandpa's shoulders, Benjamin, with one wondrous gasp, touched—the ancient Smile.

Then, as if something were wrong, he touched his own lips, his gums, his teeth.

"Stick your head in, boy," said Grandpa. "See if he *bites!*"

Somehow the weeks ran on, the summer slid by, the books piled up, the sketches got laid out in Benjamin's room: blueprints of bones, dental charts from the Jurassic and Cretaceous.

"Also, the My Gracious," mused Grandpa, peeking in. "What's *that?*"

"Sockdolager paintings by Mr. Knight, the man who sees through time, and *paints* it!"

Just then a pebble rapped the upstairs window.

"Hey!" cried some voices down below. "Ben!"

Ben went to the window, raised it, and yelled through the screen. "What do you want?"

It was one of the boys on the lawn below. "Ain't seen you in weeks, Ben. Come on swimming."

"Who cares," said Ben.

"Making ice cream, later, at Jim's."

"Who cares!" Ben slammed the window and turned to find a further aghast grandparent.

"I thought banana ice cream turned you mad with desire," said the old one. "You haven't been out in weeks! Hold 'er, Newt." Grandpa delved into his pockets, sorted

papers, found an announcement. "I know a way! Read!"
Benjamin grabbed and read:

SUNDAY SERMON. FIRST BAPTIST.
10:00 A.M.*VISITING PREACHER*:
ELLSWORTH CLUE. SERMON:
THE YEARS BEFORE ADAM,
THE TIME BEFORE EVE

"Boy!" cried Benjamin. "This mean what I *think* it means? Can we go?"
"Here's your hat, what's your hurry," said Gramps.

It not being Sunday, there was a long wait. But Sunday morning early, Ben came dragging Grandpa down the street to the First Baptist.

And, sure enough, inside, the Beast Tamer, Reverend Clue, launched behemoths smackdab into his sermon, fished for whales, caught leviathans, shadowed the Deeps, and ended with a thundering herd which, if they were not dinosaurs, were sulphurous bestial first cousins. And all waiting in the fiery pits for Christian boys who might fall through and land in that delightful burning place.

Or so it seemed to Benjamin, who sat upright for the first church hour in his life, his eyes ungummed, his mouth unyawned.

The Reverend Clue, seeing the boy's bright smile and flashing eyes, checked him out from time to time as he raved on through a genealogy of beasts with Lucifer the black goatherd on the swarm.

At noon, the congregation, released from the Bestiary, and smoking from its rollercoaster slide through Hell, staggered out blinking-blind into full sunlight, knowing more about prehistoric butcheries than they had wished to know. All, that is, save Benjamin, who found the Reverend, stunned by his own rhetoric, and yanked his hand like a pumphandle, hoping more miracles of beast might squirt out of the holy man's mouth.

"Gosh, Reverend, that was great! The monsters!"

"Don't hold a candle to monsters like men, however," said the Reverend, trying to keep his sermon on the track.

Benjamin was not to be veered.

"I liked the part about wishing making it so. That true?"

The Reverend almost flinched under the boy's signal-fire blink.

"Why—"

"I mean," said Benjamin, "if someone wishes for something bad enough, it comes true?"

"If," said Grandpa, arriving to save the Reverend from his offspring, "if you give to the poor, say proper prayers, do homework neat, clean up your room. . . ."

Grandpa ran out of gas.

"That's a goshawful lot," said Benjamin, glancing from precipice of Grandpa to high mesa of Reverend Clue. "What do I do first?"

"The Lord wakes us each day to our work, son. Me to mine: reverending. You to yours: being a boy, willing and ready to wish and become!"

"Wish and become!" Benjamin chortled, his face afire. "Wish and become."

"After chores, however, boy, after chores."

But Benjamin, pepped up and vinegary-full, ran, stopped, came back, not hearing.

"Reverend. God invented those beasts, right?"

"Why, bless you, son. He *did*."

"You ever figure *why*?"

Grandpa put his hand on Benjamin's shoulder, but Ben, he didn't feel it. "I mean, why would God make dinosaurs and then lose them?"

"He works in mysterious ways—"

"Too mysterious for me," said Ben, bluntly. "Wouldn't it be great, if we had our very own dinosaur here in Green Town, Illinois, arrived again, and never lost? The bones are great. But the *real* thing, wouldn't that be *swell*?"

"I have a partiality to the monsters, myself," admitted the Reverend.

"Do you think God will ever invent them again?"

The conversation, the Reverend could see, was headed for the bog. He did not intend to sink there.

"All I know for sure is, if you die and go to Hell, the beasts'll *be* there, or a facsimile, waiting for you."

Benjamin beamed.

"Almost makes dying worth*while!*"

"Son," said the Reverend.

But the boy was gone, running.

Benjamin raced home to cram his stomach and feed his eyes. He laid a dozen books spread-eagled on the floor and laughed quietly, with joy.

There they were, the beasts of all the Bible generations and beyond into the Deeps. That had a fine ring to it. The boy went around saying it from Sunday dinner at two until Sunday naptime at four. Deeps. Deeps. Take a long breath. Breathe it out. Deeps.

And brontosaur begat pteranodon and pteranodon begat tyrannosaur and tyrannosaur begat the great midnight kites—pterodactyls! and . . . so on and so forth and et cetera.

And as he turned the pages of the great fat family Text there were the leviathans and the creatures of time, and when you moved over into Hell and took a room there, why there was Dante pointing to this terror and that nightmare and this snake and that coiling serpent, all first aunts and dreadful uncles of Lost Time and strange blood and odd flesh. It made your socks crawl up your ankles and your ears drop to see the like! Oh, lost upon the Earth, but try to come again, good pets who once lay by the foot of God and got tossed out for fouling the carpet, sound! Oh, great lap-beasts of rolling mist and boiling fogs, whose voices are the trump of time that cracks the gates and lets the horrors forth, sound! Cry!

Moan from the—Deeps.

His lips moved as he slept and the sun moved shadows across his bed in the late afternoon. Twitch. Murmur. Whisper. . . .

Deeps.

Good old animal Rex had his name changed by Benjamin the next day. From then on he was known as just plain Dog.

About three days after that, whining, Dog limped shivering out of the house, and disappeared.

"Where's Dog?" asked Grandpa, who looked in the cellar, the attic (what would a dog do in an attic? nothing to dig up *there!*), and the front yard. "Dog!" he called. "Dog?" asking a huge question to the clear breeze that crossed the lawn in place of the best friend animal. And at last, "Dog? What you doing there?"

For Dog was across the street, lying in the middle of a field of clover and weeds, an empty lot where no one had ever built or lived.

After about half an hour of calling, Grandpa lit his pipe and strolled over. He stood above Dog looking down. Dog looked up with a dreadful sorrow in his eyes.

"What you doing here, boy?"

Dog, being inarticulate, could not answer, but thumped his tail and lowered his ears and whined. The world was cursed, that was for sure, and he wasn't coming home.

Crossing back over, leaving Dog behind in the safe grass, Grandpa beheld something like the Manatee of an old sailing vessel on the porch. It was of course Grandma, breasting the noon wind, a spatula in her hand. She waved it at Dog.

"I hope you didn't take him anything to eat!?"

"Lands, no," said Grandpa, turning to look back at the dog, who now slunk, quavering, in the clover. "Why?"

"He's been in the icebox."

"How'd a dog do that?"

"The Lord hasn't told me, but there's food all over the floor. Hamburger I had put aside for today, gone. And messes of dropped burger and bone all around."

"Dog wouldn't do that! Let me *see!*"

Grandma gave a final, tart, mean wave of her spatula at the dog across the street, who promptly retreated another ten yards in the grass. Then she went, a parade of one, in and through the house to thrust her spatula at the floor, which was indeed a jigsaw puzzle of strewn food.

"You mean to say that creature knows how to unlock that icebox lever? Don't make sense."

"You think it was some boarder walking in his or her sleep?"

Grandpa crouched and began picking up the bits. "Been chewed all right. No other dog around here I know. Well, now. Well."

"You better have a talk with him. Tell Dog, one more incident like this and its rice-stuffed Dog for dinner Sunday! Outa the way, I've got the mop!"

The mop descended and Grandpa, in retreat, tried one curse or another, of a gentle sort, and went back out to the porch.

"Dog!" he called. "There's lots to discuss!"

But Dog, he lay low.

The list of disasters leaning into cataclysm grew. It seemed as if the Four Horsemen of the Apocalypse were galloping over the roofs, knocking apples to rot off the trees. Grandpa suspicioned that somehow he had been invited to a dark Mardi Gras, the end results of which might be bed-wetting, slammed doors, fallen cakes, and printing errors.

For the facts were these: Dog came back to visit from across the street, but no sooner back, left again, his hair brushed in all directions, his eyes hard-boiled eggs of apprehension. With him went Mr. Wyneski, faithful

boarder and all-time town barber. Mr. Wyneski hinted
he had had it up to about here, gill-high, with Benjamin
grinding his teeth at the table.

Why, he further hinted, didn't Grandpa haul in the
town dentist to remove the boy's thrashing-machine bi-
cuspids, or loan the boy out to a wheat mill and let him
earn his keep grinding flour!

Mr. Wyneski, in sum, would not be combed smooth.
He went early and stayed late at his barber shop, coming
back on occasion for his afternoon nap, but turning
around and leaving as soon as he saw that Dog was still
in the meadow.

Worse, the boarders were busy rocking forty times a
minute, as though they were rushing down a road, instead of lolling along at the easy mileage of about once
every twenty seconds like they did in the good old days of
just last month.

That rocking, and the sight of the cat coming down off
the roof, would be Mr. Wyneski's barometer. If he saw
them, he'd vault in for some of Grandma's sorely missed
noontime shortcake.

Oh, about the cat. Starting about the same time as
Dog went to weave clover through his twitching pelt, the
cat clawed its way to the roof where it skittered nights,
yowling, and making a grand hieroglyph of graffiti on
the tarpaper, which Grandpa tried to decipher each
morn.

Mr. Wyneski even volunteered to prop a ladder and
fetch the cat down so he could sleep nights. This done,
the cat, in terror of some invisible force, ran right back
up, roof-writing along the way, to jump shivering at any
leaf that fell or wind that blew as Benjamin watched
from a window in his room. . . .

Grandpa finally settled for putting cream and tuna
up in the rain-trough where, starved, the cat shivered
down once a day to feed and then panicked back up as far
as its sanity allowed.

With the barber hiding out in his shop, Dog in the
meadow, cat on roof, Grandpa began to misset type down

at his printing palace. Some of the misprints were words he had often heard boilermakers or railroad workmen use, but which had never fired off his own tongue.

On the day when he typeset Hot Dog as Hot Damn, Grandpa tore off his green celluloid visor, crumpled his ink-stained apron and came home early to dandelion wine before, as well as after, dinner.

"It's a crisis for sure."

"Eh?" said Grandma, late on the front porch.

Grandpa hadn't realized he had spilled the beans. He covered his lapse by pouring more wine in his mouth.

"Nothing, nothing," he said.

But it was something. Listening, he thought he heard the source of the Apocalypse upstairs:

Benjamin bicuspiding the silence, grinding the summer to a lurching, locomotive halt. All with his teeth. They were getting sharper. . . .

This was the final night. It had to be, or else, in one more day, the cat would tear itself down the middle of the roof, Dog would bone-rot in the grass, and the boarders be carried off to the nut bin, talking in tongues.

Half in, half out of an irritable sleep, Grandpa awoke and sat bolt upright.

He had *heard* something. *Really* heard it this time.

It was a sound from an old movie, but he couldn't remember where or what, and was forgetful about the when.

But it stirred the fuzz in his ears and raised the hackles of his soul and bumped the flesh along his ankles like a strange new growth of hair.

He saw his toes, down at the far edge of the bed, like small mice peering out at the dreadful night, and pulled them in.

He heard the cat dancing around in hysteria on the high attic roof. Dog, far over in the empty lot meadow, bayed at the moon, but there *was* no moon!

Grandpa held his breath and listened. But there was

no further sound, no echo, no ricochet off the soundboard courthouse tower and back.

He turned over and was about to sink back into the black tar for a billion-year snooze when he thought: strange! wait! why tar? why billion years? why snooze!?

That got Grandpa bolt upright, out of bed, into the cellar, clothing himself in bathrobe on the way; clothing himself, in basement, with one sip of dandelion wine, and while he was at it, how about three?

In the library, finishing his libation, he heard a last, smaller sound, and trudged up to Benjamin's room.

Benjamin lay with a fever sweating his brow, resembling nothing more nor less than a lover fresh from a multifaceted encounter with a fine lady off a Greek vase. Grandpa laughed to himself. Come now, old man, he thought, he's only a boy—

He turned and almost stumbled over the litter of books put out on the floor, or laid open for sightseeing, on the shelves.

"Why, Benjamin," he gasped. "I didn't know you had so much, so many! Lord!"

For there in a panoply, a bas-relief, a tapestry, a museum explosion, were half a hundred books, spread-eagled and butterflied, with dinosaurs grinning, lurching, touching primeval mists with fingerprinting claws. While others rode the kite skies with whistle-drumming membrances, or periscoped up with long boa-constrictor necks from smoking bogs, or grasped at the teeming sky as they sank to vanish in tombs of black tar, lost in the billion years that had summoned the old man awake.

"Never seen the like," he whispered.

And he never had.

The faces. The bodies. The great graffiti-etching spider feet, or the ham feet or the ballet feet, take your pick, find your shoe. And the mad scientist-surgeon's claws, scalpeling delicate sandwiches of meat, pâtés, minces from fellow beasts. Here a triceratops raked the jungle sands with his upside-down horny fronds, knocked over

44   RAY BRADBURY

and yanked to oblivion by Tyrannosaurus Rex. There sailed a grand brontosaur, like an arrogant Titanic, headed for unseen collisions with flesh, time, weather, and bergs headed south overland in an Age of Ice. Above all, the stringless kites, the warplane nightmare pterodactyls, scissoring the mists, kettle-drumming the winds, flirting and shuttering like ugly fans, like books of horror, in the always-murdered and so always-drying crimson sky.

"So. . . ."

Grandpa bent to shut the books, firmly, grimly.

He went down the stairs to fetch new books, his own. He brought them back up and opened them and laid them out on the floor, the shelves, the bed.

He stood for a moment in the center of the room and then he heard himself whisper:

"What do you want to be, when you grow up?"

The boy had somehow heard in his fevered sleep. His head thrashed on his pillow. One hand flailed softly, reaching for the dream.

"I—"

The old man waited.

"I," murmured the boy. "I'm . . . growing . . . *now.*"

"What?"

"Now . . . now," whispered Benjamin.

Shadows moved on his lips, his cheeks.

Grandpa bent and stared.

"Why, Ben," he said, hoarsely. "You been grinding your teeth. And—"

A trickle of blood rimmed the edges of the boy's tight mouth. A bright drop fell and dissolved into the pillow case.

"Enough's enough."

Grandpa sat and took Benjamin's restless hands quietly but firmly in his own. He leaned his head forward and began to recommend:

"Sleep, Ben, sleep. Sleep, but . . . *listen here!*"

Benjamin turned his head this way and that, squirming, perspiration flowing down his face, but—listened.

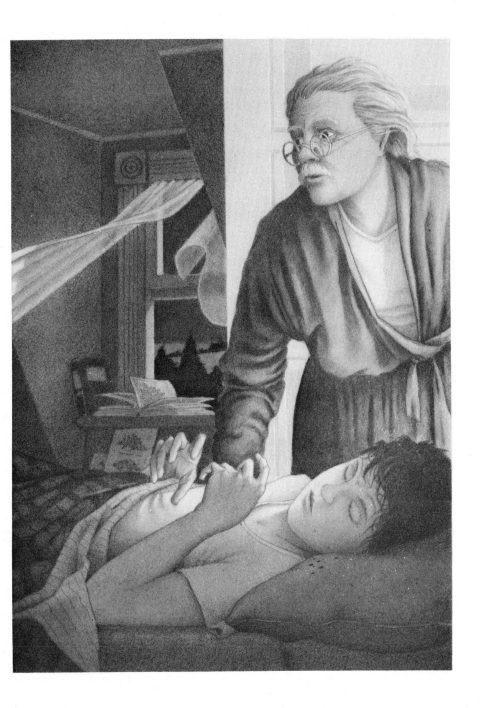

"Now," said Grandpa quietly, "what you're up to, or I think you're up to, won't do. I'm not sure what it is, and I never want to know, but whatever it is must stop."

He paused for a moment, rallied himself, and then went on:

"The magazines get shut, the books go back to the library, the chicken stays whole in the icebox, the dog comes home from across the street, the cat comes down off the roof, Mr. Wyneski rejoins us at table, and the boarders stop stealing my dandelion wine to get them through a night of strange sounds.

"Now listen even closer. No more Field Museums, no more bones, no more dental charts of old smiles, no more shadow-shows on walls of cinema houses with great ghosts of super-primeval times. This is your Grandpa talking and advising and telling you his love, but firmly warning you, for certain-sure: *no more!*

"Otherwise the whole house will fall. The attic will crash down through the bedrooms, through the dining room, the kitchen, into the cellar to ruin the summer preserves and Grandma and me and the boarders with it.

"We can't have that, can we? Shall I tell you what we can have? Look *there*.

"In the night, when I'm gone, when you get up to go to the bathroom and see what I've laid out on the floor, all around, open and waiting. There you'll find the beast, the monster, something for you to be part of, something that shouts and roars and runs and eats fire and shortens time.

"A different beast? Yes, but a grand and glorious one you can surely fit and grow into. Listen to me in your sleep, Ben, and during the night before you sleep again, prowl *these* books, these pages, these pictures. Yes?"

The old man turned to look at the books he had brought and laid out like a spell on the bedroom floor.

Pictures of fiery locomotives lay waiting for perusal, belching flames and rushing soots across night country, great animals shot from Hell. And atop the dark beasts, the locomotive engineers leaned out to dog the firewinds, smiling their locomotive-happy smiles.

"There's an engineer's cap here, Benjamin," whispered Grandpa. "Grow your head, grow your brains, but especially, grow your dreams into it. There's enough wildness there for any boy, and a lifetime of travel and glory."

The old man prowled over the flaming machines, envious of their pistoned beauties, imagining the great primeval sounds they made.

"You hear me, Ben? You *listening*?"

The boy stirred, the boy moaned, in his sleep.

Grandpa said, "I dearly hope so, boy."

The bedroom door shut. The old man was gone. The house slept. Far away, a train wailed in the night. Benjamin turned a final time in his sleep, and his fever broke. The perspiration faded on his luminous brow. A quiet wind from the open window flicked the open pages of all the books, revealing iron beast after iron beast after iron. . . .

The next morning, Sunday, Benjamin came late to breakfast. He had slept long and hard and full of dreams, prayers, wishes, bindle sticks of this, old bones of that, flesh and blood of something lost and beyond, vanished pasts, promising futures.

He came slowly down the stairs, looking fresh-washed and brand-new.

The few boarders still at table, when they saw him, got up, napkined their mouths, and left in what they hoped didn't look like a hurry.

Grandpa, at his end of the table, pretended to read the international news on the front page of the newspaper, but all the while his eyes, above the headlines, watched as Benjamin sat down, picked up his knife and fork and waited for Grandma to place his stack of pancakes drowned in liquid sun.

"Morning, Benjamin," said Grandma, sailing back out to her chores.

Benjamin waited, his mouth shut. He seemed to be thinking about something, wondering, pondering, eyes half shut.

"Benjamin," said Grandpa, behind the paper, "good morning."

Benjamin still pondered over his shut and secret mouth.

The silent table waited.

Grandpa could not help leaning forward. He found that his legs were tensed. When the boy's mouth opened, would there be a terrible-ancient cry, a dreadful shriek, announcing the birth of young Benjamin's new career? Would his smile be a fence of daggers and his tongue a field of blood?

Grandpa glanced sidewise.

Dog, home from the meadow, had just trotted into the kitchen to wolf a biscuit. Cat, down from the roof, was slicking its whiskers of cream, leaning against Grandma's right ankle. Mr. Wyneski? Would he soon be trotting up the front steps again?

"Ben," said Grandpa at last. "Besides a dinosaur, what do you want to be, when you grow up?"

Benjamin raised his head, smiled, and showed plain ordinary nice little corn-kernel teeth. His plain little old tongue moved quietly across his lips. From his lap he raised and put on a striped engineer's cap which, while large, fitted very well.

A train sighed off across the land, running on the rim of morning. Benjamin listened to it, nodded, sighed, perked some of its sound in his throat, and said:

"I think you know, Grandpa. I think you know."

And, not grinding his teeth anymore, he poured breakfast in. Grandpa could not but do likewise. Dog and cat watched from the door.

Grandma, oblivious to it all, trotted in with more hotcakes, trotted out for more syrup.

RAY BRADBURY

A Sound of Thunder

The sign on the wall seemed to quaver under a film of sliding warm water. Eckels felt his eyelids blink over his stare, and the sign burned in this momentary darkness:

TIME SAFARI, INC.
SAFARIS TO ANY YEAR
IN THE PAST.
YOU NAME THE ANIMAL.
WE TAKE YOU THERE.
YOU SHOOT IT.

A warm phlegm gathered in Eckels' throat; he swallowed and pushed it down. The muscles around his mouth formed a smile as he put his hand slowly out upon the air, and in that hand waved a check for ten thousand dollars at the man behind the desk.

"Does this safari guarantee I come back alive?"

"We guarantee nothing," said the official, "except the dinosaurs." He turned. "This is Mr. Travis, your Safari Guide in the Past. He'll tell you what and where to shoot. If he says no shooting, no shooting. If you disobey instructions, there's a stiff penalty of another ten thousand

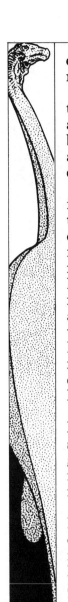

dollars, plus possible government action, on your return."

Eckels glanced across the vast office at a mass and tangle, a snaking and humming of wires and steel boxes, at an aurora that flickered now orange, now silver, now blue. There was a sound like a gigantic bonfire burning all of Time, all the years and all the parchment calendars, all the hours piled high and set aflame.

A touch of the hand and this burning world, on the instant, beautifully reverses itself. Eckels remembered the wording in the advertisements to the letter. Out of chars and ashes, out of dust and coals, like golden salamanders, the old years, the green years, might leap; roses sweeten the air, white hair turn Irish-black, wrinkles vanish; all, everything fly back to seed, flee death, rush down to their beginnings, suns rise in western skies and set in glorious easts, moons eat themselves opposite to the custom, all and everything cupping one in another like Chinese boxes, rabbits into hats, all and everything returning to the fresh death, the seed death, the green death, to the time before the beginning. A touch of a hand might do it, the merest touch of a hand.

"Hell and damn," Eckels breathed, the light of the Machine on his thin face. "A real Time Machine." He shook his head. "Makes you think. If the election had gone badly yesterday, I might be here now running away from the results. Thank God, Keith won. He'll make a fine President of the United States."

"Yes," said the man behind the desk. "We're lucky. If Deutscher had gotten in, we'd have the worst kind of dictatorship. There's an anti-everything man for you, a militarist, anti-Christ, antihuman, anti-intellectual. People called us up, you know, joking but not joking. Said if Deutscher became President they wanted to go live in 1492. Of course it's not our business to conduct Escapes, but to form Safaris. Anyway, Keith's President now. All you got to worry about is—"

"Shooting my dinosaur." Eckels finished it for him.

"A Tyrannosaurus Rex. The damndest monster in

history. Sign this release. Anything happens to you, we're not responsible. Those dinosaurs are hungry."

Eckels flushed angrily. "Trying to scare me!"

"Frankly, yes. We don't want anyone going who'll panic at the first shot. Six Safari leaders were killed last year and a dozen hunters. We're here to give you the damndest thrill a *real* hunter ever asked for. Traveling you back sixty million years to bag the biggest damned game in all Time. Your personal check's still there. Tear it up."

Mr. Eckels looked at the check for a long time. His fingers twitched.

"Good luck," said the man behind the desk. "Mr. Travis, he's all yours."

They moved silently across the room, taking their guns with them, toward the Machine, toward the silver metal and the roaring light.

First a day and then a night and then a day and then a night, then it was day-night-day-night-day. A week, a month, a year, a decade. A.D. 2055. A.D. 2019. 1999! 1957! Gone! The Machine roared.

They put on their oxygen helmets and tested the intercoms.

Eckels swayed on the padded seat, his face pale, his jaw stiff. He felt the trembling in his arms and he looked down and found his hands tight on the new rifle. There were four other men in the Machine. Travis, the Safari leader; his assistant, Lesperance; and two other hunters, Billings and Kramer. They sat looking at each other, and the years blazed between them.

"Can these guns get a dinosaur cold?" Eckels felt his mouth saying.

"If you hit them right," said Travis on the helmet radio. "Some dinosaurs have two brains, one in the head, another far down the spinal column. We stay away from those. That's stretching luck. Put your first two shots into the eyes, if you can, blind them, and go back into the

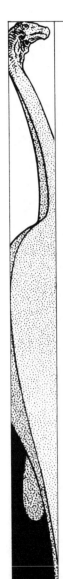

brain."

The Machine howled. Time was a film run backwards. Suns fled and ten million moons fled after them. "Good God," said Eckels. "Every hunter that ever lived would envy us today. This makes Africa seem like Illinois."

The Machine slowed; its scream fell to a murmur. The Machine stopped.

The sun stopped in the sky.

The fog that had enveloped the Machine blew away and they were in an old time, a very old time indeed, three hunters and two Safari Heads with their blue metal guns across their knees.

"Christ isn't born yet," said Travis. "Moses has not gone to the mountain to talk with God. The Pyramids are still in the earth, waiting to be cut out and put up. *Remember* that. Alexander, Caesar, Napoleon, Hitler—none of them exists."

The men nodded.

"That"—Mr. Travis pointed—"is the jungle of sixty million two thousand and fifty-five years before President Keith."

He indicated a metal path that struck off into green wilderness, over steaming swamp, among giant ferns and palms.

"And that," he said, "is the Path, laid by Time Safari for your use. It floats six inches above the earth. Doesn't touch so much as one grass blade, flower, or tree. It's an antigravity metal. Its purpose is to keep you from touching this world of the Past in any way. Stay on the Path. Don't go off it. I repeat. *Don't go off.* For *any* reason! If you fall off, there's a penalty. And don't shoot any animal we don't okay."

"Why?" asked Eckels.

They sat in the ancient wilderness. Far birds' cries blew on a wind, and the smell of tar and an old salt sea, moist grasses, and flowers the color of blood.

"We don't want to change the Future. We don't belong here in the Past. The government doesn't *like* us here. We have to pay big graft to keep our franchise. A Time Machine is damn finicky business. Not knowing it, we might kill an important animal, a small bird, a roach, a flower even, thus destroying an important link in a growing species."

"That's not clear," said Eckels.

"All right," Travis continued, "say we accidentally kill one mouse here. That means all the future families of this one particular mouse are destroyed, right?"

"Right."

"And all the families of the families of the families of that one mouse! With a stamp of your foot, you annihilate first one, then a dozen, then a thousand, a million, a *billion* possible mice!"

"So they're dead," said Eckels. "So what?"

"So what?" Travis snorted quietly. "Well, what about the foxes that'll need those mice to survive? For want of ten mice, a fox dies. For want of ten foxes, a lion starves. For want of a lion, all manner of insects, vultures, infinite billions of life forms are thrown into chaos and destruction. Eventually it all boils down to this: fifty-nine million years later, a cave man, one of a dozen on the *entire world*, goes hunting wild boar or saber-toothed tiger for food. But you, friend, have *stepped* on all the tigers in that region. By stepping on *one* single mouse. So the cave man starves. And the cave man, please note, is not just *any* expendable man, no! He is an *entire future nation*. From his loins would have sprung ten sons. From *their* loins one hundred sons, and thus onward to a civilization. Destroy this one man, and you destroy a race, a people, an entire history of life. It is comparable to slaying some of Adam's grandchildren. The stamp of your foot, on one mouse, could start an earthquake, the effects of which could shake our Earth and destinies down through Time, to their very foundations. With the death of that one cave man, a billion others yet unborn are throttled in the womb. Perhaps Rome never rises on its seven hills. Perhaps Europe is forever a dark forest, and only Asia waxes healthy and teeming. Step on a mouse

Wm Stout '82

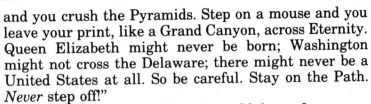

and you crush the Pyramids. Step on a mouse and you leave your print, like a Grand Canyon, across Eternity. Queen Elizabeth might never be born; Washington might not cross the Delaware; there might never be a United States at all. So be careful. Stay on the Path. *Never* step off!"

"I see," said Eckels. "Then it wouldn't pay for us even to touch the *grass*?"

"Correct. Crushing certain plants could add up infinitesimally. A little error here would multiply in sixty million years, all out of proportion. Of course maybe our theory is wrong. Maybe Time *can't* be changed by us. Or maybe it can be changed only in little subtle ways. A dead mouse here makes an insect imbalance there, a population disproportion later, a bad harvest further on, a depression, mass starvation, and, finally, a change in *social* temperament in far-flung countries. Something much more subtle, like that. Perhaps only a soft breath, a whisper, a hair, pollen on the air, such a slight, slight change that unless you looked close you wouldn't see it. Who knows? Who really can say he knows? We don't know. We're guessing. But until we do know for certain whether our messing around in Time *can* make a big roar or a little rustle in History, we're being damned careful. This Machine, this Path, your clothing and bodies, were sterilized, as you know, before the journey. We wear these oxygen helmets so we can't introduce our bacteria into an ancient atmosphere."

"How do we know which animals to shoot?"

"They're marked with red paint," said Travis. "Today, before our journey, we sent Lesperance here back with the Machine. He came to this particular era and followed certain animals."

"Studying them?"

"Right," said Lesperance. "I track them through their entire existence, noting which of them lives longest. Not long. How many times they mate. Not often. Life's short. When I find one that's going to die when a tree falls on him, or one that drowns in a tar pit, I note the exact hour, minute, and second. I shoot a paint bomb. It leaves a red patch on his hide. We can't miss it. Then I correlate our arrival in the Past so that we meet the Monster not more than two minutes before he would have died anyway. You see how *careful* we are?"

"But if you came back this morning in Time," said Eckels eagerly, "you must have bumped into *us*, our Safari! How did it turn out? Was it successful? Did all of us get through—alive?"

Travis and Lesperance gave each other a look.

"That'd be a paradox," said the latter. "Time doesn't permit that sort of mess—a man meeting himself. When such occasions threaten, Time steps aside. Like an airplane hitting an air pocket. You felt the Machine jump just before we stopped? That was us passing ourselves on the way back to the Future. We saw nothing. There's no way of telling *if* this expedition was a success, *if* we got our Monster, or whether all of us—meaning *you*, Mr. Eckels—got out alive."

Eckels smiled palely.

"Cut that," said Travis sharply. "Everyone on his feet!"

They were ready to leave the Machine.

The jungle was high and the jungle was broad and the jungle was the entire world forever and forever. Sounds like music and sounds like flying tents filled the sky, and those were pterodactyls soaring with cavernous gray wings, gigantic bats out of a delirium and a night fever. Eckels, balanced on the narrow Path, aimed his rifle playfully.

"Stop that!" said Travis. "Don't even aim for fun, damn it! If your gun should go off—"

Eckels flushed. "Where's our Tyrannosaurus?"

Lesperance checked his wristwatch. "Up ahead. We'll bisect his trail in sixty seconds. Look for the red paint, for Christ's sake. Don't shoot till we give the word. Stay on the Path. *Stay on the Path!*"

They moved forward in the wind of morning.

"Strange," murmured Eckels. "Up ahead, sixty mil-

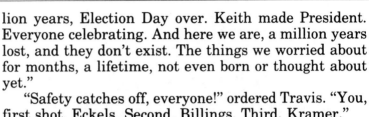

lion years, Election Day over. Keith made President. Everyone celebrating. And here we are, a million years lost, and they don't exist. The things we worried about for months, a lifetime, not even born or thought about yet."

"Safety catches off, everyone!" ordered Travis. "You, first shot, Eckels. Second, Billings. Third, Kramer."

"I've hunted tiger, wild boar, buffalo, elephant, but Jesus, this is *it*," said Eckels. "I'm shaking like a kid."

"Ah," said Travis.

Everyone stopped.

Travis raised his hand. "Ahead," he whispered. "In the mist. There he is. There's His Royal Majesty now."

The jungle was wide and full of twitterings, rustlings, murmurs, and sighs.

Suddenly it all ceased, as if someone had shut a door.

Silence.

A sound of thunder.

Out of the mist, one hundred yards away, came Tyrannosaurus Rex.

"Jesus God," whispered Eckels.

"Shh!"

It came on great oiled, resilient, striding legs. It towered thirty feet above half of the trees, a great evil god, folding its delicate watchmaker's claws close to its oily reptilian chest. Each lower leg was a piston, a thousand pounds of white bone, sunk in thick ropes of muscle, sheathed over in a gleam of pebbled skin like the mail of a terrible warrior. Each thigh was a ton of meat, ivory, and steel mesh. And from the great breathing cage of the upper body, those two delicate arms dangled out front, arms with hands which might pick up and examine men like toys, while the snake neck coiled. And the head itself, a ton of sculptured stone, lifted easily upon the sky. Its mouth gaped, exposing a fence of teeth like daggers. Its eyes rolled, ostrich eggs, empty of all expression save hunger. It closed its mouth in a deadly grin. It ran, its pelvic bones crushing aside trees and bushes, its tal-oned feet clawing damp earth, leaving prints six inches deep wherever it settled its weight. It ran with a gliding ballet step, far too poised and balanced for its ten tons. It moved into a sunlit area warily, its beautiful reptile hands feeling the air.

"My God!" Eckels twitched his mouth. "It could reach up and grab the Moon."

"Shh!" Travis jerked angrily. "He hasn't seen us yet."

"It can't be killed." Eckels pronounced this verdict quietly, as if there could be no argument. He had weighed the evidence and this was his considered opin-ion. The rifle in his hands seemed a cap gun. "We were fools to come. This is impossible."

"Shut up!" hissed Travis.

"Nightmare."

"Turn around," commanded Travis. "Walk quietly to the Machine. We'll remit one-half your fee."

"I didn't realize it would be this *big*," said Eckels. "I miscalculated, that's all. And now I want out."

"It *sees* us!"

"There's the red paint on its chest!"

The Thunder Lizard raised itself. Its armored flesh glittered like a thousand green coins. The coins, crusted with slime, steamed. In the slime, tiny insects wriggled, so that the entire body seemed to twitch and undulate, even while the Monster itself did not move. It exhaled. The stink of raw flesh blew down the wilderness.

"Get me out of here," said Eckels. "It was never like this before. I was always sure I'd come through alive. I had good guides, good safaris, and safety. This time, I figured wrong. I've met my match and admit it. This is too much for me to get hold of."

"Don't run," said Lesperance. "Turn around. Hide in the Machine."

"Yes." Eckels seemed to be numb. He looked at his feet as if trying to make them move. He gave a grunt of helplessness.

"Eckels!"

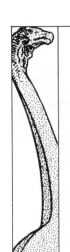

He took a few steps, blinking, shuffling.

"Not *that* way!"

The Monster, at the first motion, lunged forward with a terrible scream. It covered one hundred yards in four seconds. The rifles jerked up and blazed fire. A windstorm from the beast's mouth engulfed them in the stench of slime and old blood. The Monster roared, teeth glittering with sun.

Eckels, not looking back, walked blindly to the edge of the Path, his gun limp in his arms, stepped off the Path, and walked, not knowing it, into the jungle. His feet sank into green moss. His legs moved him, and he felt alone and remote from the events behind.

The rifles cracked again. Their sound was lost in shriek and lizard thunder. The great lever of the reptile's tail swung up, lashed sideways. Trees exploded in clouds of leaf and branch. The Monster twitched its jeweler's hands down to fondle at the men, to twist them in half, to crush them like berries, to cram them into its teeth and its screaming throat. Its boulder-stone eyes leveled with the men. They saw themselves mirrored. They fired at the metallic eyelids and the blazing black iris.

Like a stone idol, like a mountain avalanche, Tyrannosaurus fell. Thundering, it clutched trees, pulled them with it. It wrenched and tore the metal Path. The men flung themselves back and away. The body hit, ten tons of cold flesh and stone. The guns fired. The Monster lashed its armored tail, twitched its snake jaws, and lay still. A fount of blood spurted from its throat. Somewhere inside, a sac of fluids burst. Sickening gushes drenched the hunters. They stood, red and glistening.

The thunder faded.

The jungle was silent. After the avalanche, a green peace. After the nightmare, morning.

Billings and Kramer sat on the pathway and threw up. Travis and Lesperance stood with smoking rifles, cursing steadily.

In the Time Machine, on his face, Eckels lay shivering. He had found his way back to the Path, climbed into the Machine.

Travis came walking, glanced at Eckels, took cotton gauze from a metal box, and returned to the others, who were sitting on the Path.

"Clean up."

They wiped the blood from their helmets. They began to curse too. The Monster lay, a hill of solid flesh. Within, you could hear the sighs and murmurs as the furthest chambers of it died, the organs malfunctioning, liquids running a final instant from pocket to sac to spleen, everything shutting off, closing up forever. It was like standing by a wrecked locomotive or a steam shovel at quitting time, all valves being released or levered light. Bones cracked; the tonnage of its own flesh, off-balance, dead weight, snapped the delicate forearms, caught underneath. The meat settled, quivering.

Another cracking sound. Overhead, a gigantic tree branch broke from its heavy mooring, fell. It crashed upon the dead beast with finality.

"There." Lesperance checked his watch. "Right on time. That's the giant tree that was scheduled to fall and kill this animal originally." He glanced at the two hunters. "You want the trophy picture?"

"What?"

"We can't take a trophy back to the Future. The body has to stay right here where it would have died originally so the insects, birds, and bacteria can get at it, as they were intended to. Everything in balance. The body stays. But we *can* take a picture of you standing near it."

The two men tried to think, but gave up, shaking their heads.

They let themselves be led along the metal Path. They sank wearily into the Machine cushions. They gazed back at the ruined Monster, the stagnating mound, where already strange reptilian birds and golden insects were busy at the steaming armor.

A sound on the floor of the Time Machine stiffened them. Eckels sat there, shivering.

"I'm sorry," he said at last.

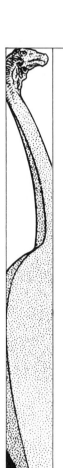

"Get up!" cried Travis.

Eckels got up.

"Go out on that Path alone," said Travis. He had his rifle pointed. "You're not coming back in the Machine. We're leaving you here!"

Lesperance seized Travis' arm. "Wait—"

"Stay out of this!" Travis shook his hand away. "This son of a bitch nearly killed us. But it isn't *that* so much. Hell, no. It's his *shoes*! Look at them! He ran off the Path. My God, that *ruins* us! Christ knows how much we'll forfeit! Tens of thousands of dollars of insurance. We guarantee no one leaves the Path. He left it. Oh, the damn fool! I'll have to report to the government. They might revoke our license to travel. God knows *what* he's done to Time, to History!"

"Take it easy, all he did was kick up some dirt."

"How do we *know*?" cried Travis. "We don't know anything! It's all a damn mystery! Get out there, Eckels!"

Eckels fumbled at his shirt. "I'll pay anything. A hundred thousand dollars!"

Travis glared at Eckels' checkbook and spat. "Go out there. The Monster's next to the Path. Stick your arms up to your elbows in his mouth. Then you can come back with us."

"That's unreasonable!"

"The Monster's dead, you yellow bastard. The bullets! The bullets can't be left behind. They don't belong in the Past; they might change something. Here's my knife. Dig them out!"

The jungle was alive again, full of the old tremorings and bird cries. Eckels turned slowly to regard that primeval garbage dump, that hill of nightmares and terror. After a long time, like a sleepwalker, he shuffled out along the Path.

He returned, shuddering, five minutes later, his arms soaked and red to the elbows. He held out his hands. Each held a number of steel bullets. Then he fell. He lay where he fell, not moving.

"You didn't have to make him do that," said Lesperance.

"Didn't I? It's too early to tell." Travis nudged the still body. "He'll live. Next time he won't go hunting game like this. Okay." He jerked his thumb wearily at Lesperance. "Switch on. Let's go home."

1492. 1776. 1812.

They cleaned their hands and faces. They changed their caking shirts and pants. Eckels was up and around again, not speaking. Travis glared at him for a full ten minutes.

"Don't look at me," cried Eckels. "I haven't done anything."

"Who can tell?"

"Just ran off the Path, that's all, a little mud on my shoes—what do you want me to do—get down and pray?"

"We might need it. I'm warning you, Eckels, I might kill you yet. I've got my gun ready."

"I'm innocent. I've done nothing!"

1999. 2000. 2055.

The Machine stopped.

"Get out," said Travis.

The room was there as they had left it. But not the same as they had left it. The same man sat behind the same desk. But the same man did not quite sit behind the same desk.

Travis looked around swiftly. "Everything okay here?" he snapped.

"Fine. Welcome home!"

Travis did not relax. He seemed to be looking at the very atoms of the air itself, at the way the sun poured through the one high window.

"Okay, Eckels, get out. Don't ever come back."

Eckels could not move.

"You heard me," said Travis. "What're you *staring* at?"

Eckels stood smelling the air, and there was a thing

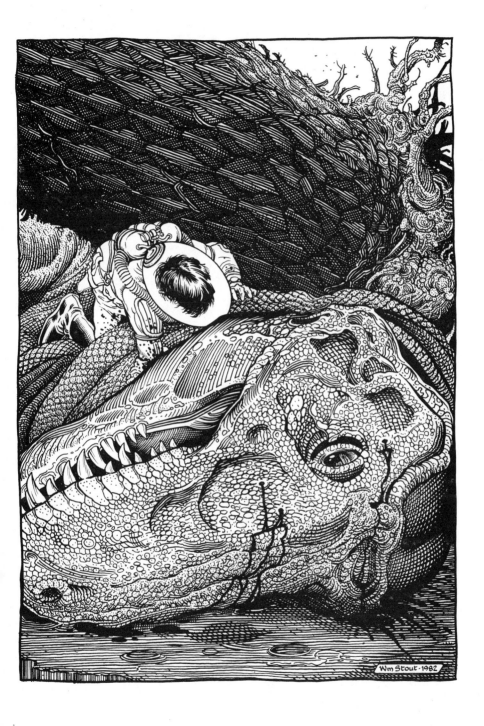

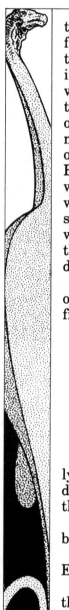

to the air, a chemical taint so subtle, so slight, that only a faint cry of his subliminal senses warned him it was there. The colors, white, gray, blue, orange, in the wall, in the furniture, in the sky beyond the window, were. . . were. . . And there was a *feel*. His flesh twitched. His hands twitched. He stood drinking the oddness with the pores of his body. Somewhere, someone must have been screaming one of those whistles that only a dog can hear. His body screamed silence in return. Beyond this room, beyond this wall, beyond this man who was not quite the same man seated at this desk that was not quite the same desk. . . lay an entire world of streets and people. What sort of world was it now; there was no telling. He could feel them moving there, beyond the walls, almost, like so many chess pieces blown in a dry wind. . . .

But the immediate thing was the sign painted on the office wall, the same sign he had read earlier today on first entering.

Somehow, the sign had changed:

TYME SEFARI INC.
SEFARIS TU ANY YEER EN THE PAST.
YU NAIM THE ANIMALL.
WEE TAEK YU THAIR.
YU SHOOT ITT.

Eckels felt himself fall into a chair. He fumbled crazily at the thick slime on his boots. He held up a clod of dirt, trembling. "No, it *can't* be. Not a *little* thing like that. No!"

Embedded in the mud, glistening green and gold and black, was a butterfly, very beautiful, and very dead.

"Not a little thing like *that*! Not a butterfly!" cried Eckels.

It fell to the floor, an exquisite thing, a small thing that could upset balances and knock down a line of small dominoes and then big dominoes and then gigantic dominoes, all down the years across Time. Eckels' mind

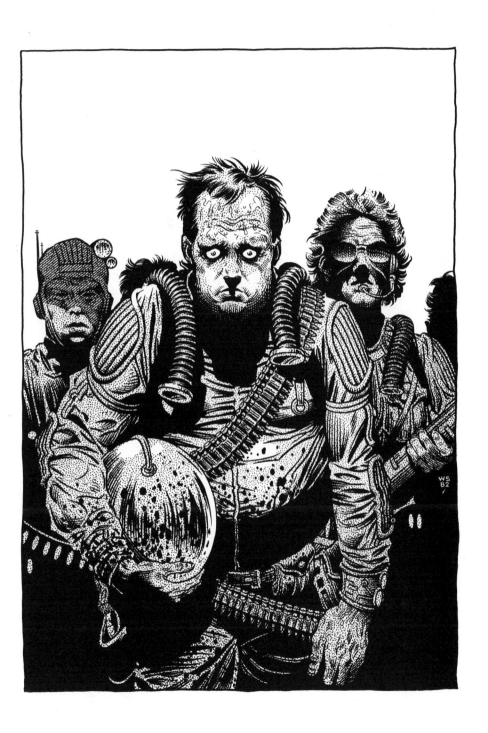

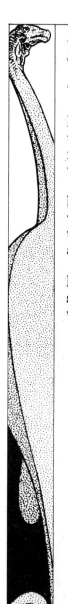

whirled. It *couldn't* change things. Killing one butterfly couldn't be *that* important! Could it?

His face was cold. His mouth trembled, asking: "Who—who won the presidential election yesterday?"

The man behind the desk laughed. "You joking? You know damn well. Deutscher, of course. Who else? Not that damn weakling Keith. We got an iron man now, a man with guts, by God!" The official stopped. "What's wrong?"

Eckels moaned. He dropped to his knees. He scrabbled at the golden butterfly with shaking fingers. "Can't we," he pleaded to the world, to himself, to the officials, to the Machine, "can't we take it *back*, can't we *make* it alive again? Can't we start over? Can't we—"

He did not move. Eyes shut, he waited, shivering. He heard Travis breathe loud in the room; he heard Travis shift his rifle, click the safety catch, and raise the weapon.

There was a sound of thunder.

Lo, the Dear, Daft Dinosaurs!

Holy smoke, can I be dreaming?
What's that waltzing up the strand?
Dinosaurs from deeps are streaming,
Come to jumble-jog the land!
On the dappled brim of Brighton
Allosaurus ept doth waft,
In the tidal gluts they frighten,
Slap-tap-tapping fore and aft.

86   RAY BRADBURY

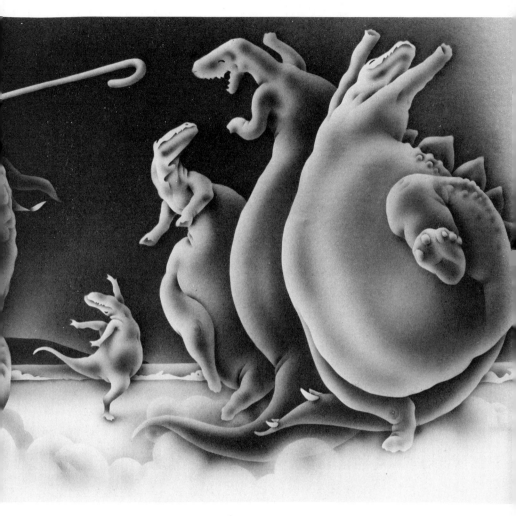

Where the moonlight plows to harrow
Sea-beasts waken from their tar,
Brontosaurs in flesh and marrow
Waltz where asphalt maidens are.
Locked in creosote gone mellow,
Fallen females grab a snooze,
Dead triceratops and fellow
Dream the dank primeval ooze,

Now upheaved from the Jurassic,
Or perhaps a bit Cretaceous?
Poised "en-pointe" and purely classic,
Fabrosaurus glides most gracious,
Roused, all smiles, for this occasion,
Hence to caper down the Mall.
Balanchinic celebration!
Architectures rumba, fall.

See the tide-flats jolt and shiver,
As the earthquaked beasts rebound,
Then do soft-shoed "Swanee River"
On their tribal stamping ground.
Pterodactyls, high and kiting,
Fly above them, staring down,
As the brontosaurs cease fighting
So's to rigadoon the town.

DINOSAUR TALES 89

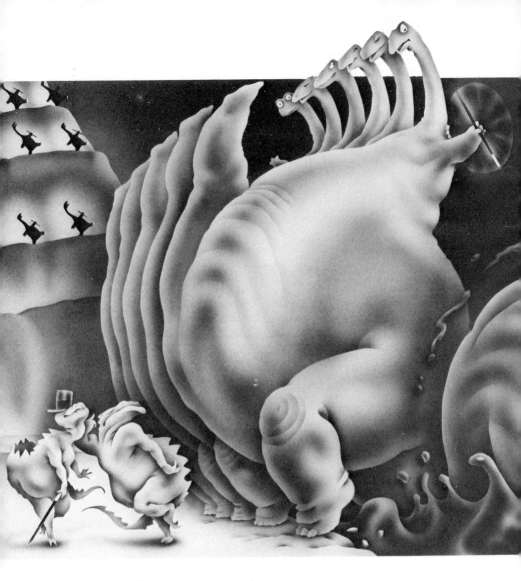

Now the sauropods, a twosome,
Whirling, freeze. *She* genuflects.
As her ripe smile, sharply gruesome,
Wins Tyrannosaurus Rex.
Forward, backward, backward, forward
From the sumpholes at a trot,
Rex and sabertooths swim shoreward,
Joined in Herculean gavotte.

RAY BRADBURY

Like an avalanche in Limbo
Ninety tons jeté in pairs,
Spinosaurus, legs akimbo,
Dares to bow, then falls downstairs.
Their toe-dancing sets example,
Battle Hymns of Time their tune,
Grapes of Wrath they turmoil-trample,
'Neath a rapture-ruptured moon.

Now the dancing duos, many,
Stegosaurs from Yonkers, York,
Iguanodons from Allegheny
Stop their waltzing, pull the cork.
Locomotive-loud, these charmers,
Thunder steams and, steaming, stride,
In their chain-mail-hammered armors
Titan fleas do, hopping, hide.
Start with flea and then, wide-grinning,
Jaw the mists to yearn through yeast
Till your Tyrant Lizard, spinning
Dines a dental-smiling feast.
Where the tar pools, sucking, sinking,
Where dark ages glut and gloat,
There the sad beasts, gasping, drinking,
Drown their woes in creosote.
Lost to us along the shore-wild,
Sunk in pits, they quit the cause,
For each deft, daft dinosaur child?
From the tide flats: loud applause!
Critics and more critic-fellas,
Shout, "Bravo, tyrannosaur!"
Judge a ton of tarantellas;
Praise the Beasts. But *damn* the Tar.

The Fog Horn

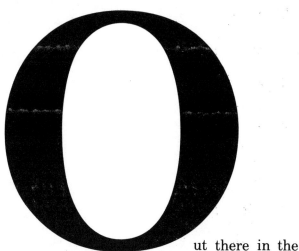

Out there in the cold water, far from land, we waited every night for the coming of the fog, and it came, and we oiled the brass machinery and lit the fog light up in the stone tower. Feeling like two birds in the gray sky, McDunn and I sent the light touching out, red, then white, then red again, to eye the lonely ships. And if they did not see our light, then there was always our Voice, the great deep cry of our Fog Horn shuddering through the rags of mist to startle the gulls away like decks of scattered cards and make the waves turn high and foam.

"It's a lonely life, but you're used to it now, aren't you?" asked McDunn.

"Yes," I said. "You're a good talker, thank the Lord."

"Well, it's your turn on land tomorrow," he said, smiling, "to dance the ladies and drink gin."

"What do you think about, McDunn, when I leave you out here alone?"

"On the mysteries of the sea." McDunn lit his pipe. It was a quarter past seven of a cold November evening, the heat on, the light switching its tail in two hundred directions, the Fog Horn bumbling in the high throat of the tower. There wasn't a town for a hundred miles down the coast, just a road which came lonely through dead

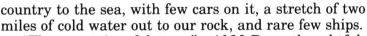

country to the sea, with few cars on it, a stretch of two miles of cold water out to our rock, and rare few ships.

"The mysteries of the sea," said McDunn thoughtfully. "You know, the ocean's the biggest damned snowflake ever? It rolls and swells a thousand shapes and colors, no two alike. Strange. One night, years ago, I was here alone, when all of the fish of the sea surfaced out there. Something made them swim in and lie in the bay, sort of trembling and staring up at the tower light going red, white, red, white across them so I could see their funny eyes. I turned cold. They were like a big peacock's tail, moving out there until midnight. Then, without so much as a sound, they slipped away, the million of them was gone. I kind of think maybe, in some sort of way, they came all those miles to worship. Strange. But think how the tower must look to them, standing seventy feet above the water, the God-light flashing out from it, and the tower declaring itself with a monster voice. They never came back, those fish, but don't you think for a while they thought they were in the Presence?"

I shivered. I looked out at the long gray lawn of the sea stretching away into nothing and nowhere.

"Oh, the sea's full." McDunn puffed his pipe nervously, blinking. He had been nervous all day and hadn't said why. "For all our engines and so-called submarines, it'll be ten thousand centuries before we set foot on the real bottom of the sunken lands, in the fairy kingdoms there, and know *real* terror. Think of it, it's still the year 300,000 Before Christ down there. While we've paraded around with trumpets, lopping off each other's countries and heads, they have been living beneath the sea twelve miles deep and cold in a time as old as the beard of a comet."

"Yes, it's an old world."

"Come on. I got something special I been saving up to tell you."

We ascended the eighty steps, talking and taking our time. At the top, McDunn switched off the room lights so there'd be no reflection in the plate glass. The great eye of the light was humming, turning easily in its oiled socket. The Fog Horn was blowing steadily, once every fifteen seconds.

"Sounds like an animal, don't it?" McDunn nodded to himself. "A big lonely animal crying in the night. Sitting here on the edge of ten billion years calling out to the Deeps, I'm here, I'm here, I'm here. And the Deeps *do* answer, yes, they do. You been here now for three months, Johnny, so I better prepare you. About this time of year," he said, studying the murk and fog, "something comes to visit the lighthouse."

"The swarm of fish, like you said?"

"No, this is something else. I've put off telling you because you might think I'm daft. But tonight's the latest I can put it off, for if my calendar's marked right from last year, tonight's the night it comes. I won't go into detail, you'll have to see it yourself. Just sit down there. If you want, tomorrow you can pack your duffel and take the motorboat in to land and get your car parked there at the dinghy pier on the cape and drive on back to some little inland town and keep your lights burning nights. I won't question or blame you. It's happened three years now, and this is the only time anyone's been here with me to verify it. You wait and watch."

Half an hour passed with only a few whispers between us. When we grew tired waiting, McDunn began describing some of his ideas to me. He had some theories about the Fog Horn itself.

"One day many years ago, a man walked along and stood in the sound of the ocean on a cold sunless shore and said, 'We need a voice to call across the water, to warn ships; I'll make one. I'll make a voice like all of time and all of the fog that ever was; I'll make a voice that is like an empty bed beside you all night long, and like an empty house when you open the door, and like trees in autumn with no leaves. A sound like the birds flying south, crying, and a sound like November wind and the sea on the hard, cold shore. I'll make a sound that's so alone that no one can miss it, that whoever

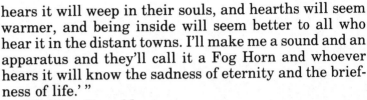

hears it will weep in their souls, and hearths will seem warmer, and being inside will seem better to all who hear it in the distant towns. I'll make me a sound and an apparatus and they'll call it a Fog Horn and whoever hears it will know the sadness of eternity and the briefness of life.' "

The Fog Horn blew.

"I made up that story," said McDunn quietly, "to try to explain why this thing keeps coming back to the lighthouse every year. The Fog Horn calls it, I think, and it comes. . . . "

"But—" I said.

"Sssst!" said McDunn. "There!" He nodded out to the Deeps.

Something was swimming toward the lighthouse tower.

It was a cold night, as I have said; the high tower was cold, the light coming and going, and the Fog Horn calling and calling through the raveling mist. You couldn't see far and you couldn't see plain, but there was the deep sea moving on its way about the night earth, flat and quiet, the color of gray mud, and here were the two of us alone in the high tower, and there, far out at first, was a ripple, followed by a wave, a rising, a bubble, a bit of froth. And then, from the surface of the cold sea came a head, a large head, dark-colored, with immense eyes, and then a neck. And then—not a body—but more neck and more! The head rose a full forty feet above the water on a slender and beautiful dark neck. Only then did the body, like a little island of black coral and shells and crayfish, drip up from the subterranean. There was a flicker of tail. In all, from head to tip of tail, I estimated the monster at ninety feet or a hundred feet.

I don't know what I said. I said something.

"Steady, boy, steady," whispered McDunn.

"It's impossible!" I said.

"No, Johnny, *we're* impossible. *It's* like it always was ten million years ago. *It* hasn't changed. It's *us* and the land that have changed, become impossible. *Us!*"

It swam slowly and with a great dark majesty out in the icy waters, far away. The fog came and went about it, momentarily erasing its shape. One of the monster eyes caught and held and flashed back our immense light, red, white, red, white, like a disk held high and sending a message in primeval code. It was as silent as the fog through which it swam.

"It's a dinosaur of some sort!" I crouched down, holding to the stair rail.

"Yes, one of the tribe."

"But they died out!"

"No, only hid away in the Deeps. Deep, deep down in the deepest Deeps. Isn't *that* a word now, Johnny, a real word, it says so much: the Deeps. There's all the coldness and darkness and deepness in the world in a word like that."

"What'll we do?"

"Do? We got our job, we can't leave. Besides, we're safer here than in any boat trying to get to land. That thing's as big as a destroyer and almost as swift."

"But here, why does it come *here*?"

The next moment I had my answer.

The Fog Horn blew.

And the monster answered.

A cry came across a million years of water and mist. A cry so anguished and alone that it shuddered in my head and my body. The monster cried out at the tower. The Fog Horn blew. The monster roared again. The Fog Horn blew. The monster opened its great toothed mouth, and the sound that came from it was the sound of the Fog Horn itself. Lonely and vast and far away. The sound of isolation, a viewless sea, a cold night, apartness. That was the sound.

"Now," whispered McDunn, "do you know why it comes here?"

I nodded.

"All year long, Johnny, that poor monster there lying far out, a thousand miles at sea, and twenty miles deep maybe, biding its time, perhaps it's a million years old,

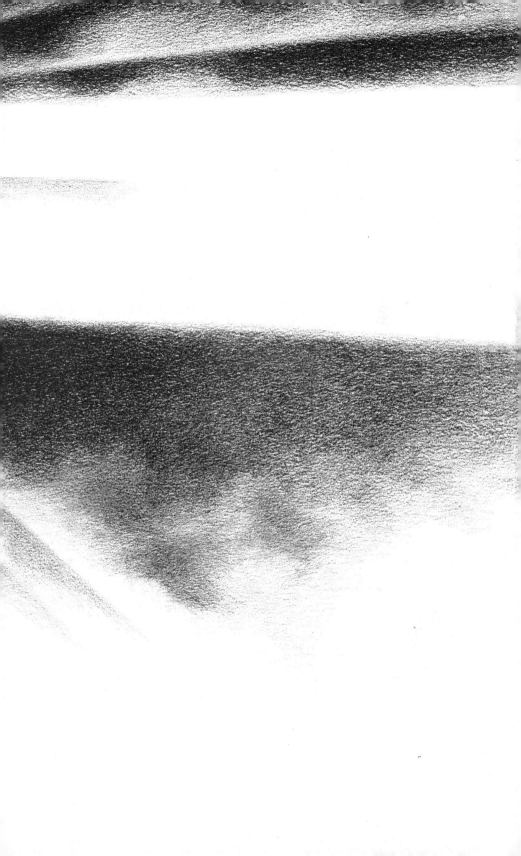

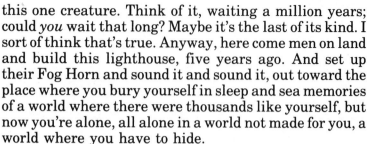

this one creature. Think of it, waiting a million years; could *you* wait that long? Maybe it's the last of its kind. I sort of think that's true. Anyway, here come men on land and build this lighthouse, five years ago. And set up their Fog Horn and sound it and sound it, out toward the place where you bury yourself in sleep and sea memories of a world where there were thousands like yourself, but now you're alone, all alone in a world not made for you, a world where you have to hide.

"But the sound of the Fog Horn comes and goes, comes and goes, and you stir from the muddy bottom of the Deeps, and your eyes open like the lenses of two-foot cameras and you move, slow, slow, for you have the ocean sea on your shoulders, heavy. But that Fog Horn comes through a thousand miles of water, faint and familiar, and the furnace in your belly stokes up, and you begin to rise, slow, slow. You feed yourself on great slakes of cod and minnow, on rivers of jellyfish, and you rise slow through the autumn months, through September when the fogs started, through October with more fog and the horn still calling you on, and then, late in November, after pressurizing yourself day by day, a few feet higher every hour, you are near the surface and still alive. You've got to go slow; if you surfaced all at once you'd explode. So it takes you all of three months to surface, and then a number of days to swim through the cold waters to the lighthouse. And there you are, out there, in the night, Johnny, the biggest damn monster in creation. And here's the lighthouse calling to you, with a long neck like your neck sticking way up out of the water, and a body like your body, and, most important of all, a voice like your voice. Do you understand now, Johnny, do you understand?"

The Fog Horn blew.

The monster answered.

I saw it all, I knew it all—the million years of waiting alone, for someone to come back who never came back. The million years of isolation at the bottom of the sea, the insanity of time there, while the skies cleared of reptile-birds, the swamps dried on the continental lands, the sloths and sabertooths had their day and sank in tar pits, and men ran like white ants upon the hills.

The Fog Horn blew.

"Last year," said McDunn, "that creature swam round and round, round and round, all night. Not coming too near, puzzled, I'd say. Afraid, maybe. And a bit angry after coming all this way. But the next day, unexpectedly, the fog lifted, the sun came out fresh, the sky was as blue as a painting. And the monster swam off away from the heat and the silence and didn't come back. I suppose it's been brooding on it for a year now, thinking it over from every which way."

The monster was only a hundred yards off now, it and the Fog Horn crying at each other. As the lights hit them, the monster's eyes were fire and ice, fire and ice.

"That's life for you," said McDunn. "Someone always waiting for someone who never comes home. Always someone loving some thing more than that thing loves them. After a while you want to destroy whatever that thing is, so it can't hurt you no more."

The monster was rushing at the lighthouse.

The Fog Horn blew.

"Let's see what happens," said McDunn.

He switched the Fog Horn off.

The ensuing minute of silence was so intense that we could hear our hearts pounding in the glassed area of the tower, could hear the slow greased turn of the light.

The monster stopped and froze. Its great lantern eyes blinked. Its mouth gaped. It gave a sort of rumble, like a volcano. It twitched its head this way and that, as if to seek the sounds now dwindled off into the fog. It peered at the lighthouse. It rumbled again. Then its eyes caught fire. It reared up, threshed the water, and rushed at the tower, its eyes filled with angry torment.

"McDunn!" I cried. "Switch on the horn!"

McDunn fumbled with the switch. But even as he flicked it on, the monster was rearing up. I had a glimpse of its gigantic paws, fishskin glittering in webs between

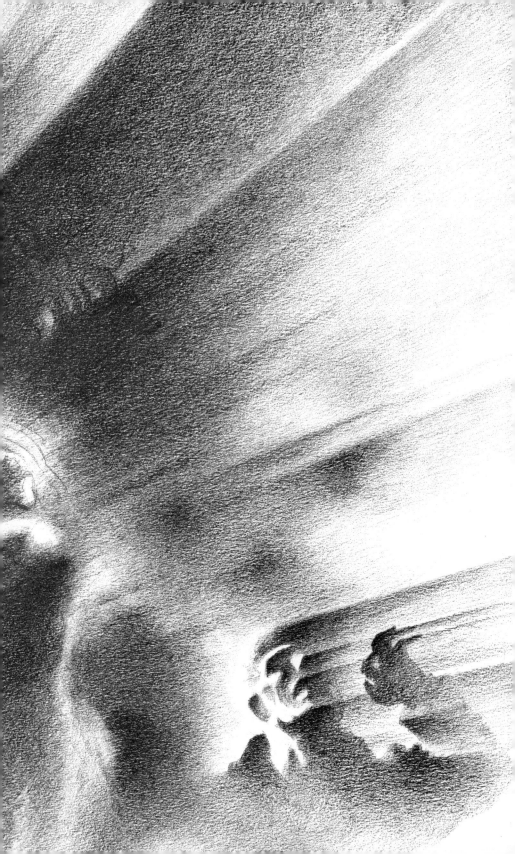

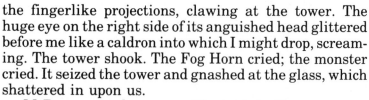

the fingerlike projections, clawing at the tower. The huge eye on the right side of its anguished head glittered before me like a caldron into which I might drop, screaming. The tower shook. The Fog Horn cried; the monster cried. It seized the tower and gnashed at the glass, which shattered in upon us.

McDunn seized my arm. "Downstairs!"

The tower rocked, trembled, and started to give. The Fog Horn and the monster roared. We stumbled and half fell down the stairs. "Quick!"

We reached the bottom as the tower buckled down toward us. We ducked under the stairs into the small stone cellar. There were a thousand concussions as the rocks rained down; the Fog Horn stopped abruptly. The monster crashed upon the tower. The tower fell. We knelt together, McDunn and I, holding tight, while our world exploded.

Then it was over, and there was nothing but darkness and the wash of the sea on the raw stones.

That and the other sound.

"Listen," said McDunn quietly. "Listen."

We waited a moment. And then I began to hear it. First a great vacuumed sucking of air, and then the lament, the bewilderment, the loneliness of the great monster, folded over and upon us, above us, so that the sickening reek of its body filled the air, a stone's thickness away from our cellar. The monster gasped and cried. The tower was gone. The light was gone. The thing that had called to it across a million years was gone. And the monster was opening its mouth and sending out great sounds. The sounds of a Fog Horn, again and again. And ships far at sea, not finding the light, not seeing anything, but passing and hearing late that night, must've thought: There it is, the lonely sound, the Lonesome Bay horn. All's well. We've rounded the cape.

And so it went for the rest of the night.

The sun was hot and yellow the next afternoon when

the rescuers came out to dig us from our stoned-under cellar.

"It fell apart, is all," said Mr. McDunn gravely. "We had a few bad knocks from the waves, and it just crumbled." He pinched my arm.

There was nothing to see. The ocean was calm, the sky blue. The only thing was a great algae stink from the green matter that covered the fallen tower stones and the shore rocks. Flies buzzed about. The ocean washed empty on the shore.

The next year they built a new lighthouse, but by that time I had a job in the little town and a wife and a good small warm house that glowed yellow on autumn nights, the doors locked, the chimney puffing smoke. As for McDunn, he was master of the new lighthouse, built to his own specifications, out of steel-reinforced concrete. "Just in case," he said.

The new lighthouse was ready in November. I drove down alone one evening late and parked my car and looked across the gray waters and listened to the new horn sounding, once, twice, three, four times a minute far out there, by itself.

The monster?

It never came back.

"It's gone away," said McDunn. "It's gone back to the Deeps. It's learned you can't love anything too much in this world. It's gone into the deepest Deeps to wait another million years. Ah, the poor thing! Waiting out there, and waiting out there, while man comes and goes on this pitiful little planet. Waiting and waiting."

I sat in my car, listening. I couldn't see the lighthouse or the light standing out in Lonesome Bay. I could only hear the Horn, the Horn, the Horn. It sounded like the monster calling.

I sat there wishing there was something I could say.

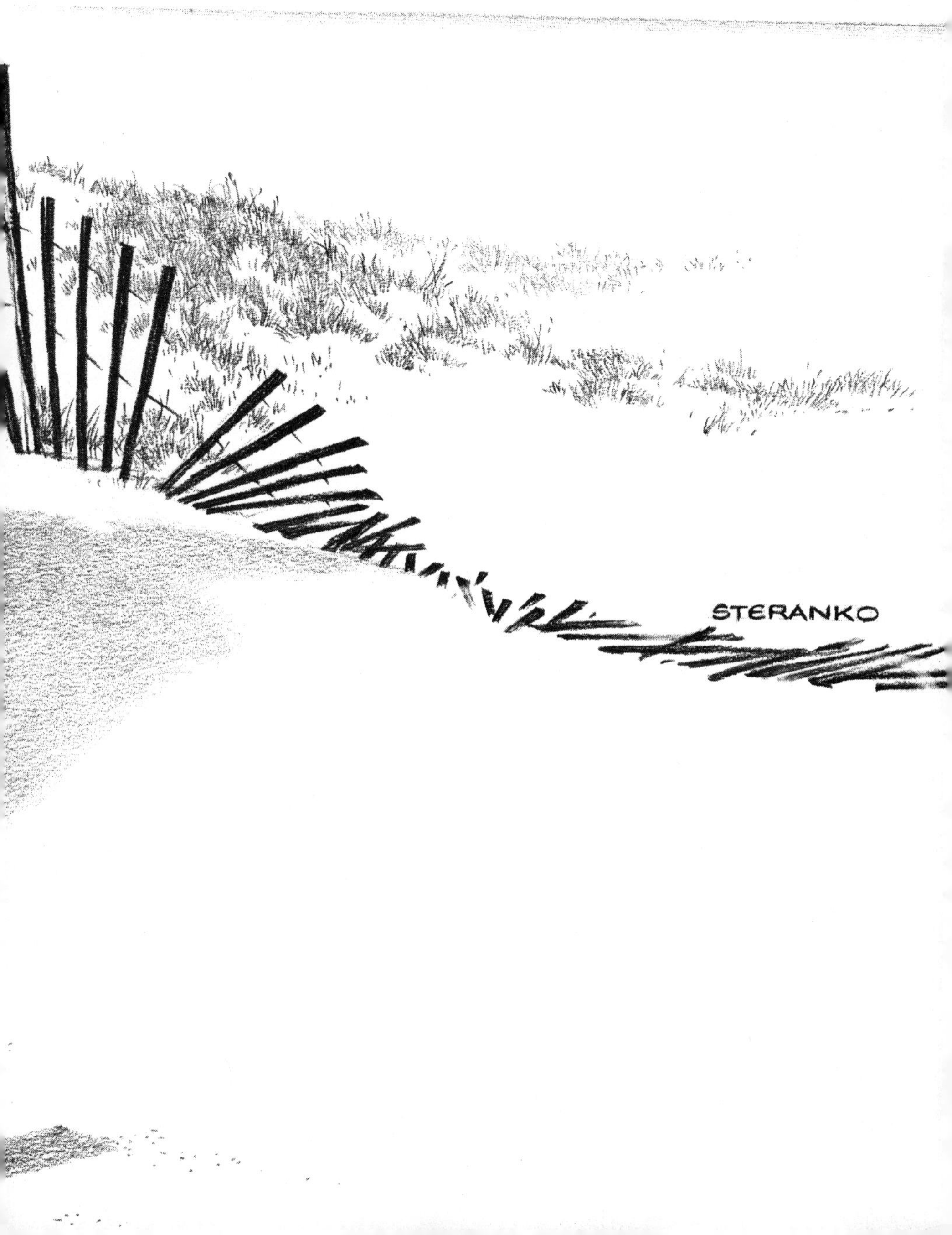
STERANKO

What If I Said: The Dinosaur's Not Dead?

What if I said:
The dinosaur's not dead?
He's outside now, all freshly arrived
Pulled up to thrive and park along the curb.
Superb!
What would you do?
Snort, laugh?
But, just in case it might be true
Would you rush out to see,
Hoping against hope
That it might be?
That's you, oh yes, that's me.
The old brutes haunt our dreams,
Our childhood schemes are bulked with them.
There lives no girl or boy
Or grown-up very old
Who wouldn't sell half their molars' gold
To meet
A dinosaur resting in mid-street
Just look!
A traffic cop pulls up beside the beast,
And while we stand there gawking,
The cop applies his pencil to a pad
And fines him for overparking!

Not mad, the cop, but legally calm
Writing it down, recording the harm
Just where and when, and then:
He hands the ticket up from underneath
And says: "Don't do it again."
The brontosaurus leaves
Ticket in teeth, but also a little smile.
In a while the cop will recall
Then whirl and run back down the mall
To stare at that place where the great beast lolled
While appalled kids stood
In exaltations
And nodded to each other:
This is horribly good.
Then each walked home with wonder and awe
To try and tell what they found and saw
That was truly great
Sorry the poor cop looked back late!
What lousy luck
To cite the likes of a primeval truck
And scribble the pad, but never wonder
Why the ancient car had a purr like thunder.
Ah, well, the parking lot is bare
No sign of the mountain anywhere
Just a few graffiti droppings on the green
That the street department will find and clean,
And even the children can't tell or show
If the beautiful beast was there, or no.

RAY BRADBURY

Tyrannosaurus Rex

**e opened**
a door on darkness. A voice cried, "Shut it!" It **was like a**
blow in the face. He jumped through. The **door banged.**
He cursed himself quietly. The voice, with **dreadful pa-**
tience, intoned, "Jesus. You Terwilliger?"

"Yes," said Terwilliger. A faint ghost **of screen**
haunted the dark theater wall to his right. **To his left, a**
cigarette wove fiery arcs in the air as **someone's lips**
talked swiftly around it.

"You're five minutes late!"

Don't make it sound like five years, **thought**
Terwilliger.

"Shove your film in the projection room **door. Let's**
move."

Terwilliger squinted.

He made out five vast loge seats that **exhaled,**
breathed heavily as amplitudes of executive life **shifted,**
leaning toward the middle loge where, almost **in dark-**
ness, a little boy sat smoking.

No, thought Terwilliger, not a boy. That's **him. Joe**
Clarence. Clarence the Great.

For now the tiny mouth snapped like a **puppet's,**
blowing smoke. "Well?"

Terwilliger stumbled back to hand the **film to the**

projectionist, who made a lewd gesture toward the loges, winked at Terwilliger and slammed the booth door.

"Jesus," sighed the tiny voice. A buzzer buzzed. "Roll it, projection!"

Terwilliger probed the nearest loge, struck flesh, pulled back and stood biting his lips.

Music leaped from the screen. His film appeared in a storm of drums:

TYRANNOSAURUS REX: THE THUNDER LIZARD.

> Photographed in stop-motion animation with miniatures created by John Terwilliger. A study in life-forms on Earth one billion years before Christ.

Faint ironic applause came softly patting from the baby hands in the middle loge.

Terwilliger shut his eyes. New music jerked him alert. The last titles faded into a world of primeval sun, mist, poisonous rain, and lush wilderness. Morning fogs were strewn along eternal seacoasts where immense flying dreams and dreams of nightmare scythed the wind. Huge triangles of bone and rancid skin, of diamond eye and crusted tooth, pterodactyls, the kites of destruction, plunged, struck prey, and skimmed away, meat and screams in their scissor mouths.

Terwilliger gazed, fascinated.

In the jungle foliage now, shiverings, creepings, insect jitterings, antennae twitchings, slime locked in oily fatted slime, armor skinned to armor, in sun glade and shadow moved the reptilian inhabiters of Terwilliger's mad remembrance of vengeance given flesh and panic taking wing.

Brontosaur, stegosaur, triceratops. How easily the clumsy tonnages of name fell from one's lips.

The great brutes swung like ugly machineries of war and dissolution through moss ravines, crushing a thousand flowers at one footfall, snouting the mist, ripping the sky in half with one shriek.

My beauties, thought Terwilliger, my little lovelies. All liquid latex, rubber sponge, ball-socketed steel articulature; all night-dreamed, clay-molded, warped and welded, riveted and slapped to life by hand. No bigger than my fist, half of them; the rest no larger than this head they sprang from.

"Good Lord," said a soft admiring voice in the dark.

Step by step, frame by frame of film, stop motion by stop motion, he, Terwilliger, had run his beasts through their postures, moved each a fraction of an inch, photographed them, moved them another hair, photographed them, for hours and days and months. Now these rare images, this eight hundred scant feet of film, rushed through the projector.

And lo! he thought. I'll never get used to it. Look! They come *alive*!

Rubber, steel, clay, reptilian latex sheath, glass eye, porcelain fang, all ambles, trundles, strides in terrible prides through continents as yet unmanned, by seas as yet unsalted, a billion years lost away. They *do* breathe. They *do* smite air with thunders. Oh, uncanny!

I feel, thought Terwilliger, quite simply, that there stands *my* Garden, and these my animal creations which I love on this Sixth Day, and tomorrow, the Seventh, I must rest.

"Lord," said the soft voice again.

Terwilliger almost answered, "Yes?"

"This is beautiful footage, Mr. Clarence," the voice went on.

"Maybe," said the man with a boy's voice.

"Incredible animation."

"I've seen better," said Clarence the Great.

Terwilliger stiffened. He turned from the screen where his friends lumbered into oblivion, from butcheries wrought on architectural scales. For the first time he examined his possible employers.

"Beautiful stuff."

This praise came from an old man who sat to himself far across the theater, his head lifted forward in amaze toward that ancient life.

"It's jerky. Look there!" The strange boy in the middle loge half rose, pointing with the cigarette in his mouth. "Hey, was *that* a bad shot? You *see?*"

"Yes," said the old man, tired suddenly, fading back in his chair. "I see."

Terwilliger crammed his hotness down upon a suffocation of swiftly moving blood.

"Jerky," said Joe Clarence.

White light, quick numerals, darkness; the music cut, the monsters vanished.

"Glad that's over." Joe Clarence exhaled. "Almost lunchtime. Throw on the next reel, Walter! That's all, Terwilliger." Silence. "Terwilliger?" Silence. "Is that dumb bunny still here?"

"Here." Terwilliger ground his fists on his hips.

"Oh," said Joe Clarence. "It's not bad. But don't get ideas about money. A dozen guys came here yesterday to show stuff as good or better than yours, tests for our new film, *Prehistoric Monster*. Leave your bid in an envelope with my secretary. Same door as you came in. Walter, what the hell are you waiting for? Roll the next one!"

In darkness, Terwilliger barked his shins on a chair, groped for and found the door handle, gripped it tight, tight.

Behind him the screen exploded: an avalanche fell in great flourings of stone, whole cities of granite, immense edifices of marble piled, broke and flooded down. In this thunder, he heard voices from the week ahead:

"We'll pay you one thousand dollars, Terwilliger."

"But I need a thousand for my equipment alone!"

"Look, we're giving you a break. Take it or leave it!"

With the thunder dying, he knew he would take, and he knew he would hate it.

Only when the avalanche had drained off to silence behind him, and his own blood had raced to the inevitable decision and stalled in his heart, did Terwilliger pull

the immensely weighted door wide to step forth into the
terrible raw light of day.

Fuse flexible spine to sinuous neck, pivot neck to
death's-head skull, hinge jaw from hollow cheek, glue
plastic sponge over lubricated skeleton, slip snake-pebbled
skin over sponge, meld seams with fire, then rear
upright triumphant in a world where insanity wakes but
to look on madness—Tyrannosaurus Rex!

The Creator's hands glided down out of arc-light sun.
They placed the granuled monster in false green summer
wilds, they waded it in broths of teeming bacterial
life. Planted in serene terror, the lizard machine basked.
From the blind heavens the Creator's voice hummed,
vibrating the Garden with the old and monotonous tune
about the footbone connected to the . . . anklebone, anklebone connected to the . . . legbone, legbone connected
to the kneebone, kneebone connected to the . . .

A door burst wide.

Joe Clarence ran in very much like an entire Cub
Scout pack. He looked wildly around as if no one were
there.

"My God!" he cried. "Aren't you set up yet? This costs
me money!"

"No," said Terwilliger dryly. "No matter how much
time I take, I get paid the same."

Joe Clarence approached in a series of quick starts
and stops. "Well, shake a leg. And make it real horrible."

Terwilliger was on his knees beside the miniature
jungle set. His eyes were on a straight level with his
producer's as he said, "How many feet of blood and gore
would you like?"

"Two thousand feet of each!" Clarence laughed in a
kind of gasping stutter. "Let's look." He grabbed the
lizard.

"Careful!"

"Careful?" Clarence turned the ugly beast in careless
and non-loving hands. "It's my monster, ain't it? The

contract—"

"The contract says you use this model for exploitation advertising, but the animal reverts to me after the film's in release."

"Holy cow." Clarence waved the monster. "That's wrong. We just signed the contracts four days ago—"

"It feels like fours years." Terwilliger rubbed his eyes. "I've been up two nights without sleep finishing this beast so we can start shooting."

Clarence brushed this aside. "To hell with the contract. What a slimy trick. It's my monster. You and your agent give me heart attacks. Heart attacks about money, heart attacks about equipment, heart attacks about—"

"This camera you gave me is ancient."

"So if it breaks, fix it; you got hands? The challenge of the shoestring operation is using the old brain instead of cash. Getting back to the point, this monster, it should've been specified in the deal, is my baby."

"I never let anyone own the things I make," said Terwilliger honestly. "I put too much time and affection in them."

"Hell, okay, so we give you fifty bucks extra for the beast, and throw in all this camera equipment free when the film's done, right? Then you start your own company. Compete with me, get even with me, right, using my own machines!" Clarence laughed.

"If they don't fall apart first," observed Terwilliger.

"Another thing." Clarence put the creature on the floor and walked around it. "I don't like the way this monster shapes up."

"You don't like *what*?" Terwilliger almost yelled.

"His expression. Needs more fire, more . . . goombah. More mazash!"

"Mazash?"

"The old bimbo! Bug the eyes more. Flex the nostrils. Shine the teeth. Fork the tongue sharper. You can *do* it! Uh, the monster ain't mine, huh?"

"Mine." Terwilliger arose.

His belt buckle was now on a line with Joe Clarence's eyes. The producer stared at the bright buckle almost hypnotically for a moment.

"God damn the goddamn lawyers!"

He broke for the door.

"Work!"

The monster hit the door a split second after it slammed shut.

Terwilliger kept his hand poised in the air from his overhand throw. Then his shoulders sagged. He went to pick up his beauty. He twisted off its head, skinned the latex flesh off the skull, placed the skull on a pedestal and, painstakingly, with clay, began to reshape the prehistoric face.

"A little goombah," he muttered. "A touch of mazash."

They ran the first film test on the animated monster a week later.

When it was over, Clarence sat in darkness and nodded imperceptibly.

"Better. But ... more horrorific, bloodcurdling. Let's scare the hell out of Aunt Jane. Back to the drawing board!"

"I'm a week behind schedule now," Terwilliger protested. "You keep coming in, change this, change that, you say, so I change it, one day the tail's all wrong, next day it's the claws—"

"You'll find a way to make me happy," said Clarence. "Get in there and fight the old aesthetic fight!"

At the end of the month they ran the second test.

"A near miss! Close!" said Clarence. "The face is just almost right. Try again, Terwilliger!"

Terwilliger went back. He animated the dinosaur's mouth so that it said obscene things which only a lip reader might catch, while the rest of the audience would think the beast was only shrieking. Then he got the clay and worked until three A.M. on the awful face.

"That's it!" cried Clarence in the projection room the next week. "Perfect! Now *that's* what I call a monster!"

He leaned toward the old man, his lawyer, Mr. Glass, and Maury Poole, his production assistant.

"You *like* my creature?" He beamed.

Terwilliger, slumped in the back row, his skeleton as long as the monsters he built, could feel the old lawyer shrug.

"You seen one monster, you seen 'em all."

"Sure, sure, but this one's special!" shouted Clarence happily. "Even *I* got to admit Terwilliger's a genius!"

They all turned back to watch the beast on the screen, in a titanic waltz, throw its razor tail wide in a vicious harvesting that cut grass and clipped flowers. The beast paused now to gaze pensively off into mists, gnawing a red bone.

"That monster," said Mr. Glass at last, squinting. "He sure looks familiar."

"Familiar?" Terwilliger stirred, alert.

"It's got such a look," drawled Mr. Glass in the dark, "I couldn't forget, from someplace."

"Natural Museum exhibits?"

"No, no."

"Maybe," laughed Clarence, "you read a book once, Glass?"

"Funny . . ." Glass, unperturbed, cocked his head, closed one eye. "Like detectives, I don't forget a face. But, that Tyrannosaurus Rex—where before did I meet *him*?"

"Who cares?" Clarence sprinted. "He's great. And all because I booted Terwilliger's behind to make him do it right. Come on, Maury!"

When the door shut, Mr. Glass turned to gaze steadily at Terwilliger. Not taking his eyes away, he called softly to the projectionist, "Walt? Walter? Could you favor us with that beast again?"

"Sure thing."

Terwilliger shifted uncomfortably, aware of some bleak force gathering in blackness, in the sharp light that shot forth once more to ricochet terror off the screen.

"Yeah. Sure," mused Mr. Glass. "I almost remember. I almost know him. But. . . *who?*"

The brute, as if answering, turned and for a disdainful moment stared across one hundred thousand million years at two small men hidden in a small dark room. The tyrant machine named itself in thunder.

Mr. Glass quickened forward, as if to cup his ear.

Darkness swallowed all.

With the film half finished, in the tenth week, Clarence summoned thirty of the office staff, technicians and a few friends to see a rough cut of the picture.

The film had been running fifteen minutes when a gasp ran through the small audience.

Clarence glanced swiftly about.

Mr. Glass, next to him, stiffened.

Terwilliger, scenting danger, lingered near the exit, not knowing why; his nervousness was compulsive and intuitive. Hand on the door, he watched.

Another gasp ran through the crowd.

Someone laughed quietly. A woman secretary giggled. Then there was instantaneous silence.

For Joe Clarence had jumped to his feet.

His tiny figure sliced across the light on the screen. For a moment, two images gesticulated in the dark: Tyrannosaurus, ripping the leg from a pteranodon, and Clarence, yelling, jumping forward as if to grapple with these fantastic wrestlers.

"Stop! Freeze it right there!"

The film stopped. The image held.

"What's wrong?" asked Mr. Glass.

"Wrong?" Clarence crept up on the image. He thrust his baby hand to the screen, stabbed the tyrant jaw, the lizard eye, the fangs, the brow, then turned blindly to the projector light so that reptilian flesh was printed on his furious cheeks. "What goes? What *is* this?"

"Only a monster, Chief."

"Monster, hell!" Clarence pounded the screen with

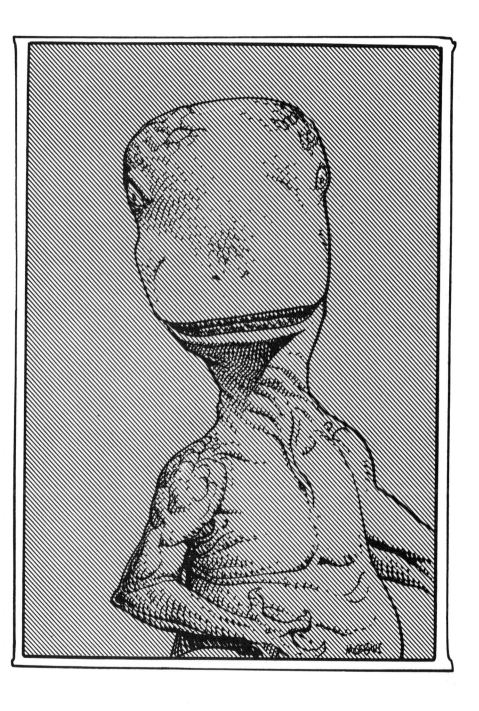

his tiny fist. "That's *me!*"

Half the people leaned forward, half the people fell back, two people jumped up, one of them Mr. Glass, who fumbled for his other spectacles, flexed his eyes and moaned, "So *that's* where I saw him before!"

"That's where you what?"

Mr. Glass shook his head, eyes shut. "That face, I *knew* it was familiar."

A wind blew in the room.

Everyone turned. The door stood open.

Terwilliger was gone.

They found Terwilliger in his animation studio cleaning out his desk, dumping everything into a large cardboard box, the Tyrannosaurus machine-toy model under his arm. He looked up as the mob swirled in, Clarence at the head.

"What did I do to deserve this!" he cried.

"I'm sorry, Mr. Clarence."

"You're sorry?! Didn't I pay you well?"

"No, as a matter of fact."

"I took you to lunches—"

"Once. I picked up the tab."

"I gave you dinner at home, you swam in my pool, and now *this*! You're fired!"

"You can't fire me, Mr. Clarence. I've worked the last week free and overtime, you forgot my check—"

"You're fired anyway, oh, you're *really* fired! You're blackballed in Hollywood. Mr. Glass!" He whirled to find the old man. "Sue him!"

"There is nothing," said Terwilliger, not looking up any more, just looking down, packing, keeping in motion, "nothing you can sue me for. Money? You never paid enough to save on. A house? Could never afford that. A wife? I've worked for people like you all my life. So wives are out. I'm an unencumbered man. There's nothing you can do to me. If you attach my dinosaurs, I'll just go hole up in a small town somewhere, get me a can of latex rubber, some clay from the river, some old steel pipe, and make new monsters. I'll buy stock film raw and cheap. I've got an old beat-up stop-motion camera. Take that away, and I'll build one with my own hands. I can do anything. And that's why you'll never hurt me again."

"You're fired!" cried Clarence. "Look at me. Don't look away. You're fired! You're fired!"

"Mr. Clarence," said Mr. Glass, quietly, edging forward. "Let me talk to him just a moment."

"So talk to him!" said Clarence. "What's the use? He just stands there with that monster under his arm and the goddam thing looks like me, so get out of the way!"

Clarence stormed out the door. The others followed.

Mr. Glass shut the door, walked over to the window and looked out at the absolutely clear twilight sky.

"I wish it would rain," he said. "That's one thing about California I can't forgive. It never really lets go and cries. Right now, what wouldn't I give for a little something from that sky? A bolt of lightning, even."

He stood silent, and Terwilliger slowed in his packing. Mr. Glass sagged down into a chair and doodled on a pad with a pencil, talking sadly, half aloud, to himself.

"Six reels of film shot, pretty good reels, half the film done, three hundred thousand dollars down the drain, hail and farewell. Out the window all the jobs. Who feeds the starving mouths of boys and girls? Who will face the stockholders? Who chucks the Bank of America under the chin? Anyone for Russian roulette?"

He turned to watch Terwilliger snap the locks on a briefcase.

"What hath God wrought?"

Terwilliger, looking down at his hands, turning them over to examine their texture, said, "I didn't know I was doing it, I swear. It came out in my fingers. It was all subconscious. My fingers do everything for me. They did *this*."

"Better the fingers had come in my office and taken me direct by the throat," said Glass. "I was never one for slow motion. The Keystone Cops, at triple speed, was my idea of living, or dying. To think a rubber monster has stepped on us all. We are now so much tomato mush, ripe for canning!"

"Don't make me feel any guiltier than I feel," said Terwilliger.

"What do you want, I should take you dancing?"

"It's just," cried Terwilliger, "he kept at me. Do this. Do that. Do it the other way. Turn it inside out, upside down, he said. I swallowed my bile. I was angry all the time. Without knowing, I must've changed the face. But right up till five minutes ago, when Mr. Clarence yelled, I didn't see it. I'll take all the blame."

"No," sighed Mr. Glass, "we should *all* have seen. Maybe we did and couldn't admit. Maybe we did and laughed all night in our sleep, when we couldn't hear. So where are we now? Mr. Clarence, he's got investments he can't throw out. Mr. Clarence right now is aching to be convinced it was all some horrible dream. Part of his ache, ninety-nine percent, is in his wallet. If you could put one percent of your time in the next hour convincing him of what I'm going to tell you next, tomorrow morning there will be no orphan children staring out of the want ads in *Variety* and *The Hollywood Reporter*. If you would go tell him—"

"Tell me *what?*"

Joe Clarence, returned, stood in the door, his cheeks still inflamed.

"What he just told me." Mr. Glass turned calmly. "A touching story."

"I'm listening!" said Clarence.

"Mr. Clarence." The old lawyer weighed his words carefully. "This film you just saw is Mr. Terwilliger's solemn and silent tribute to you."

"It's *what?*" shouted Clarence.

Both men, Clarence and Terwilliger, dropped their jaws.

The old lawyer gazed only at the wall and in a shy voice said, "Shall I go on?"

The animator closed his jaw. "If you want to."

"This film"—the lawyer arose and pointed in a single motion toward the projection room—"was done from a feeing of honor and friendship for you, Joe Clarence. Behind your desk, an unsung hero of the motion picture industry, unknown, unseen, you sweat out your lonely little life while who gets the glory? The stars. How often does a man in Atawanda Springs, Idaho, tell his wife, 'Say, I was thinking the other night about Joe Clarence—a great producer, that man'? How often? Should I tell? Never! So Terwilliger brooded. How could he present the real Clarence to the world? The dinosaur is there; boom! it hits him! This is it! he thought, the very thing to strike terror to the world, here's a lonely, proud, wonderful, awful symbol of independence, power, strength, shrewd animal cunning, the true democrat, the individual brought to its peak, all thunder and big lightning. Dinosaur: Joe Clarence. Joe Clarence: Dinosaur. Man embodied in Tyrant Lizard!"

Mr. Glass sat down, panting quietly.

Terwilliger said nothing.

Clarence moved at last, walked across the room, circled Glass slowly, then came to stand in front of Terwilliger, his face pale. His eyes were uneasy, shifting up along Terwilliger's tall skeleton frame.

"You said *that*?" he asked faintly.

Terwilliger swallowed.

"To me he said it. He's shy," said Mr. Glass. "You ever hear him say much, ever talk back? swear? anything? He likes people, he can't say. But, immortalize them? That he can do!"

"Immortalize?" said Clarence.

"What else?" said the old man. "Like a statue, only moving. Years from now people will say, 'Remember that film, *The Monster from the Pleistocene*?' And people will say, 'Sure! why?' 'Because,' the others say, 'it was the one monster, the one brute, in all Hollywood history had real guts, real personality. And why is this? Because one genius had enough imagination to base the creature on a real-life, hard-hitting, fast-thinking businessman

of A-one caliber.' You're one with history, Mr. Clarence. Film libraries will carry you in good supply. Cinema societies will ask for you. How lucky can you get? Nothing like this will ever happen to Immanuel Glass, a lawyer. Every day for the next two hundred, five hundred years, you'll be starring somewhere in the world!"

"*Every day?*" asked Clarence softly. "For the next—"

"Eight hundred, even; why not?"

"I never thought of that."

"Think of it!"

Clarence walked over to the window and looked out at the Hollywood Hills, and nodded at last.

"My God, Terwilliger," he said. "You really like me *that* much?"

"It's hard to put in words," said Terwilliger, with difficulty.

"So do we finish the mighty spectacle?" asked Glass. "Starring the tyrant terror striding the earth and making all quake before him, none other than Mr. Joseph J. Clarence?"

"Yeah. Sure." Clarence wandered off, stunned, to the door, where he said, "You know? I always *wanted* to be an actor!"

Then he went quietly out into the hall and shut the door.

Terwilliger and Glass collided at the desk, both clawing at a drawer.

"Age before beauty," said the lawyer, and quickly pulled forth a bottle of whiskey.

At midnight on the night of the first preview of *Monster from the Stone Age*, Mr. Glass came back to the studio, where everyone was gathering for a celebration, and found Terwilliger seated alone in his office, his dinosaur on his lap.

"You weren't *there?*" asked Mr. Glass.

"I couldn't face it. Was there a riot?"

"A riot? The preview cards are all superdandy extra

plus! A lovelier monster nobody saw before! So now we're talking sequels! Joe Clarence as the Tyrant Lizard in *Return of the Stone-Age Monster*, Joe Clarence and/or Tyrannosaurus Rex in, maybe, *Beast from the Old Country—*"

The phone rang. Terwilliger got it.

"Terwilliger, this is Clarence! Be there in five minutes! We've done it! Your animal! Great! Is he mine now? I mean, to hell with the contract, as a favor, can I have him for the mantel?"

"Mr. Clarence, the monster's yours."

"Better than an Oscar! So long!"

Terwilliger stared at the dead phone.

"God bless us all, said Tiny Tim. He's laughing, almost hysterical with relief."

"So maybe I know why," said Mr. Glass. "A little girl, after the preview, asked him for an autograph."

"An *autograph?*"

"Right there in the street. Made him sign. First autograph he ever gave in his life. He laughed all the while he wrote his name. Somebody knew him. There he was, in front of the theater, big as life, Rex Himself, so sign the name. So he did."

"Wait a minute," said Terwilliger slowly, pouring drinks. "That little girl . . . ?"

"My youngest daughter," said Glass. "So who knows? And who will tell?"

They drank.

"Not me," said Terwilliger.

Then, carrying the rubber dinosaur between them, and bringing the whiskey, they went to stand by the studio gate, waiting for the limousines to arrive, all lights, horns, and annunciations.

RAY BRADBURY

CONTRIBUTORS

Ray Bradbury was born in Waukegan, Illinois, in 1920. He graduated from a Los Angeles high school in 1938. His formal education ended there, but he furthered it by himself—at night in the library and by day at his typewriter. He sold newspapers on Los Angeles street corners from 1938 to 1942 a modest beginning for a man whose name would one day be synonymous with the best in science fiction. Ray Bradbury sold his first science fiction short story in 1941, and his early reputation is based on stories published in the budding science fiction magazines of that time. His work was chosen for best American short story collections in 1946, 1948 and 1952. His awards include: The O'Henry Memorial Award, The Benjamin Franklin Award in 1954 and The Aviation-Space Writer's Association Award for best space article in an American magazine in 1967. Mr. Bradbury has written for television, radio, the theater and film, and he has been published in every major American magazine. Editions of his novels and shorter fiction span several continents and languages, and he has gained worldwide acceptance for his work. His titles include: *The Martian Chronicles, Dandelion Wine, I Sing the Body Electric, The Golden Apples of the Sun, A Medicine for Melancholy, The Illustrated Man, Long After Midnight,* and *The Stories of Ray Bradbury.* His novel, *Something Wicked This Way Comes,* was recently made into a major motion picture by Walt Disney Productions, with a screenplay by the author.

William Stout is the internationally acclaimed illustrator of *The Dinosaurs,* which was the subject of a feature article in *Life.* His storyboards and production designs have been commissioned by many noted Hollywood producers.

Steranko is the award-winning graphic artist, designer and painter. He wrote and illustrated the graphic novel, *Chandler* and currently is publisher and editor of the entertainment magazine, *Prevue*.

Kenneth Smith is the popular artist and publisher of the *Phantasmagoria* group of limited edition publications and prints. His paintings have appeared on numerous book jackets and in *The Beach Boys*.

Moebius is the most respected and well-known French science fiction illustrator today. His designs were an integral part of the films *Tron* and *The Masters of Time* and he is one of the best-known and founding artists of *Metal Hurlant/Heavy Metal*.

David Wiesner is the illustrator of numerous children's books, including *Neptune's Ring* and *The Ugly Princess*. His work has been exhibited at the Metropolitan Museum of Art, the Master Eagle Gallery and the Justin Schiller Gallery.

Gahan Wilson is the popular cartoonist and illustrator of macabre books and humourous features. His cartoons have been featured in such magazines as *The New Yorker* and the *National Lampoon*, and a collection of his comic strip, *Nuts*, was published by Richard Marek.

Overton Loyd is an album cover artist, animated film designer and well-known graphic designer for the George Clinton family of recording artists. His illustrations have appeared in *The Secret*.